'Melissa' was born in England, educated in Hampshire and Indiana, and has also lived in Australia, as well as travelling extensively in the Far East. She has worked as a canteen and factory worker, model, prostitute, reflexologist and gambler, and is a second belt in the martial art of Aikido. She has two sons, has recently lived in Los Angeles and is now living in London.

MELISSA

The Harlot's Room

GRAFTON BOOKS

A Division of the Collins Publishing Group

LONDON GLASGOW
TORONTO SYDNEY AUCKLAND

Grafton Books
A Division of the Collins Publishing Group
8 Grafton Street, London W1X 3LA

Published by Grafton Books 1989

First published in Great Britain by
Chatto & Windus Ltd 1987

ISBN 0-586-20155-6

Printed and bound in Great Britain by
Collins, Glasgow

Set in Palatino

To friends at the other No. 10
and K.K. and R.B.
with thanks

Contents

1   In Which Clover Is Taught Self-Hypnosis   9
2   At Harry Hello's or Castles in Spain   16
3   At Claude Catsilk's and a Regular Life   30
4   Brixton, Tooting and Peachy Hill   51
5   The Magic Room   59
6   'You Must Be Lonely'   73
7   'Are You Frightened?'   81
8   'It Must Be Degrading'   93
9   The Green Apple   108
10 The Cricklewood Bell Snatcher   126
11 Afternoon Delight   136
12 Mothers and Gingerbread Ladies   145
13 Climax   153
14 The Pale Green Tree   167
15 Blunt Finger   185
16 Rape Scene   204
17 Happy Ending Time   217

1

In Which Clover Is Taught Self-Hypnosis

When I was about twelve I had a sudden vision of myself working as a prostitute in a vast, grey city (a city bigger and greyer than I'd ever known), living a secret life with no one knowing what or where I was. And with it came the feeling that that was the way happiness lay, the right way for me. And, as quickly as it came, it disappeared deep down inside me. This is the story of how my vision became reality.

A circle of dark men and music. Clover is sitting on the outside, breathing in smoke and drinking what she's given to drink. The language is Swahili, the music reggae, the building a high-rise council flat in Maida Vale. Clover doesn't know what the music is, she doesn't notice music, nor what sort of building it is, she doesn't see buildings. She just absorbs the sound of the language, the movements of the people, the textures of skin. She hopes sex and sleep will happen soon. A year and nineteen moves ago she was sent back to England from Australia. People see her as lovely, gentle and natural. London she hates. She feels like a visitor, not even an immigrant yet, but with immigrants she's more comfortable. Black days, black nights, black men, black mud, black clouds.

A few moves later, she is standing outside a dirty central London tube station, handing out free magazines to the early morning rush-hour crowd. It's winter. She has sandals and socks on her feet. Numb to the knees, she has not been warm enough here yet. Her right hand wears a mitten borrowed from the girl opposite. Her left hand offers magazines till it too gets numb. Then they swap mittens. She has done this two mornings a week for the last two weeks. She hopes it won't go on much longer. Clover can't stand things going on.

Rush hour finished, she takes a tube to Earl's Court and gets into bed with black coffee and Bondini. Three moves ago she was serving tea for a few weeks at a nudist club in Kent with a virgin guy from a Peckham bookshop and two randy Pekinese, and living with the owner of the camp. After three weeks she left as usual, to nothing. In London she bought *Time Out*. There was an ad from a black guy in prison in Ohio who wanted people to write to him. She wrote to him. There was also an ad for someone to assist a stage hypnotist on a cruise ship. That's how she met Bondini.

Bondini has silvery hair and wears a gold suit when he sings. He has a nice paunch which Clover likes but his lips are too thin for her, so she tries not to notice them. His accent is New York, but she doesn't know anything about accents. Bondini is going to teach her self-hypnosis so maybe they can work together on a cruise ship, teaching it to passengers. Clover wants to get out of England but she'd be stuck on the ship a long time. She sucks him for a while and is fascinated by the asymmetry of his cock.

'You should get a proper flat first,' says Bondini. 'If you had a decent flat to live in, that would give you an incentive to get a job.'

There are many things that Clover doesn't want. One of the main ones is a job. The thought of wanting a flat seems ugly to her. She has never thought about the places she has lived in. She loves people, watches them and imagines what it's like to be in their bodies. While Bondini talks she watches the strange encrustations on his finger and wonders why he has them on his arse too. He's white and his flatmate is black.

Clover thinks VD is lucky for her. Every time she's had it something nice has happened. This time she has herpes, which she hasn't had before, and Bondini is going to teach her self-hypnosis.

'Self-hypnosis helps us to tap the powers of our unconscious mind, which is far stronger and knows more than we ever dream of,' says Bondini, wiping his cock and lighting a cigarette for them both. 'But the unconscious is guarded very well by the conscious mind. We need the trick of waylaying these watchful guards and then all we need is there. Lie down and let's begin.'

She lies on the floor and relaxes as she's been told. Bondini puts all the colours of the prism in her mind. She lets them get stronger, larger, brighter.

'Imagine a peaceful scene from nature.' And a beach springs to life around Clover's body. 'Imagine you're in it.' She can hardly feel the floor now. Everything is soft and comfortable.

He tells her she can give herself commands in this state. She can do hypnosis anywhere she wants. She comes to and feels a new smile on her face.

She walks down Gloucester Road with Bondini.

'I don't feel so cold,' she says.

'It's amazing what hypnosis can do,' says Bondini.

Later Clover lies on the bed in Camden where she's been staying the last few weeks with Thora and Ted in return for collecting their kids from school. Every morning she hears them at breakfast getting angry with each other and feels sorry for them. The woman wants to live in the country and have animals. The man wants to work in the theatre. But they are not doing what they want. Clover hasn't anything to want yet.

The other day, Thora peered out of the window at the people moving in down the road.

'They look like trendies,' she said.

Clover isn't quite sure what trendies means but she thinks it might be what this couple are, so she wonders why they knock others for being the same. Every morning there is a row at breakfast. Thora frequently has to drive through the Blackwall Tunnel in the rush hour. Clover has never been to work in a rush hour and never wants to drive a car. She has to leave in a few weeks. She thinks she's very lucky this time because she has some money and somewhere to go: in the *Evening Standard* there are bed-and-breakfast places at King's Cross. Life is changing for the better.

Clover starts hypnosis by herself. She goes deeper and doesn't even feel the bed. She feels the sand strongly from her 'peaceful scene from nature'. She comes to, and it comes to her: I want to work as a prostitute. That's what I want to do. A new feeling, the strength of wanting to do something. She reads the letters from Prince in prison. She thinks she likes him from his handwriting.

Bondini has a gig in a pub, on the Isle of Dogs. On the way he's telling her how he managed to get a gig.

'I'm an old bullshitter,' he says.

Clover wonders why, if he does something as beautiful as self-hypnosis, he has to bullshit. At a bus stop he peers at a parked car.

'They look like Mafia,' he says.

In the pub, Clover breathes the smoke and waits for

the music, which she doesn't know, to finish. Roland, Bondini's flatmate, is with them. He wears a Nigerian top and remembers Clover from when he gave her his telephone number many moves ago. Bondini sits down and takes a beer. Clover listens to Roland talking about a friend. 'This chick, you know, she's a trained teacher, a really good job and she's doing cleaning, she'd rather do that, can you believe it?' Clover thinks teachers look humiliated. Cleaning at least is clean. She keeps her secret. She will do the most beautiful job of all. Later she hears Roland say, 'After all, everyone has the same aims – a house and children – don't they?' Clover thinks what a sad aim.

Next time she does self-hypnosis she gets another flash: I want to visit my kids to have access to them, but I don't want to live with them.

For the first time she knows what she wants in relation to them. Three days later an official letter arrives, forwarded from a former address, announcing a court case to prevent her from having access. She thinks it magic that just in time she should know what she wants, what to do. Ted and Thora, like most people, don't know she has kids. She visits a solicitor. She tells him she's been working as a barmaid. When people ask her what she does she always gives an answer off the top of her head. He starts dictating a letter. It must be awful for him, she thinks, working in this office five days a week and having to wear certain clothes.

Soon Bondini gets more nervous about people looking like the Mafia. He is going to live in Australia. They smoke dope together on his last evening.

'It makes everything feel amazing,' he says.

Clover doesn't think so.

When he gets a cruise-ship deal together, Clover can

join him out there. But Clover, for the first time, doesn't want to leave England just yet, not for a while, though she doesn't say so. It's her birthday and he gives her a gold-coloured ballpoint. She feels its texture. There is a golden string winding round it till it reaches the top and becomes a sphere of blue in gold with a pearl on top.

Later she flicks through *Time Out* and sees 'Attractive masseuse required. Exp. unnecessary. Full training given,' and a phone number. This sounds like it. She rings the number. And that is how she comes to meet Harry Hello.

He wears a sheepskin coat so lush and warm he doesn't need gloves. His car is warm, too, as he drives Clover to his lush, warm home on the far north outskirts of London.

In his kitchen Clover has real coffee and triangular chocolate biscuits with him. She looks at the naked wood on the walls and at his glossy black hair and smooth, soft, light-brown skin, with no gooseflesh. There are fake Victorian telephones on which Harry sells castles in Spain and toupees, but people aren't buying them because of the economy, so he's decided to start a massage parlour in the room downstairs.

'There's a physiotherapist round the corner. She'll give you an hour's training – enough so you won't damage anyone. Then you just have to wank them. It's not really prostitution.'

Clover looks at the pretty patterns on the little tables. They are onyx but she doesn't know that. She senses his need to persuade her that it's not prostitution but she wants it to be prostitution.

'I get the money for the massage. You get whatever

else you can get but I don't know anything about it –
OK?'

'Can I live in the room, too?'

'Yeah, sure.'

Clover has sex with him on his round bed for a while.
His skin compares softly to Bondini's. Then she washes
from gold-coloured bath taps. Harry gives her a lift to
the tube. He goes to put ads in newsagents' windows
and Clover collects her things, which are always nearly
packed.

2

At Harry Hello's or Castles in Spain

What was the first one like? Clover was asked much later. There wasn't a first one. To her they were an amorphous group. She hadn't had any English boyfriends. She hadn't really put sex and English guys together yet. White people – her own race – seemed alien to her. A 'they all look the same to me' sort of feeling. Their smell sometimes made her feel nervous. When she was with Indians her face felt Indian and she saw them more as individuals, and the same with West Indians. English guys became synonymous with working.

She starts with a new name. 'I'm Dawn to clients,' she tells Harry.

She goes down to the room, which is blue. She turns up a central-heating control on the wall. The room is dominated by a large high massage table and weight-lifting equipment. Harry thinks that'll make it look like a legit health studio.

Waiting for calls, she sits cosily in the room above on a gold Dralon sofa by the telephone with the largest fake gold bits on it. There are sparkling lamps on the pretty tables and a large TV set of ugly wood, and a huge wooden radiogram which Harry feeds with Frank Sinatra and Tony Bennett so he can hear it from his office on the next floor up. Clover wears her best clothes, a see-through lace purple shirt from a Walthamstow boutique owner with baby-powdered, shaved genitals, and a long swirly skirt from when she lived in

Tottenham. She has a red biro and a red notebook to write down times of appointments. When the telephone rings she picks it up first, and then Harry picks up his extension on his desk full of castle brochures and toupee pictures. Usually it's for Clover and she can feel Harry listening for a while, partly turned on and partly scared she might say too much, and what if it's the police?

'Hello. I saw your ad in the shop window. Er . . . I wonder . . . could you give me some details?'

Clover replies as Harry has instructed her. 'Hello?. Yes, it's a very nice massage and costs so much. Why don't you come along?'

Harry says, 'A business associate of mine, when I told him I was thinking of setting up a massage thing, he said, "Whatever you do, don't let them book appointments days in advance, it just never happens." And if they ask you on the phone for sex in French or anything else, say no, but make it sound like yes.' Clover prefers to answer the phone when Harry's out looking for bald heads; then she says what she wants to.

Aila, a Filipino lady, comes two days a week to clean, iron and cook. Clover sits there making occasional secret biro marks on the Dralon. She can hear Aila working in the kitchen, which leads off the lounge. Tony Bennett or Frank Sinatra is on, she doesn't know which. Harry is hovering upstairs in his office. For the first time, Clover enjoys just being. Up here she can just be, and downstairs, working, there is no one to watch her. She starts to feel peace. She absorbs all the colours. She smiles at Aila and Harry when they appear. She does self-hypnosis sitting on the sofa and more light and warmth come into her.

A letter from Bondini in Australia. 'Why don't you

train as a secretary? You could come here and get a really well-paid job.'

Clover thinks it slightly wrong that he should consider her being a secretary. It sounds a degrading occupation to her. She writes back, 'I'm in a house which has central heating and for the first time in England, I'm warm. I'm doing massage.'

On telly they say there is a fuel crisis. There are pictures of people queueing for trains which are on strike. Clover's gooseflesh has nearly disappeared. When she goes out, the cold touches her lightly and she remains warm inside herself. She goes to Portobello Road and buys a white rabbit coat. At the bus stop a guy lifts her up and cuddles her, unexpectedly. She smiles.

A letter comes from Bondini saying that he's under a deportation order for smuggling, he's on the run and she should burn all his letters.

When the guys turn up, Clover gives them a twenty-minute straight massage as the physiotherapist showed her. With her thumb circling outwards she covers the white body. She feels all their aches ease. She looks at her hands and the clients' greyish backs. She starts to like her hands. If guys ask to be kissed, or wanked, she does it, but she's careful not to offer, because Harry is scared. Sometimes she puts the mattress on the floor and they have sex on it. She sleeps on the mattress at night if she doesn't sleep in Harry's bed. It's a treat to be alone in the room. Soon she persuades Harry to get rid of the weights and dumbbells which don't fool anyone. Then there's room for a whole bed. Harry brings a portable telly from upstairs. It has a nice round aerial. She puts her cases under the stairs and nails a purple and orange beach towel over them. Harry shrieks when he sees the nail going into the wood. Now she has everything she needs. She buys tissues and Durex from the chemist. Harry doesn't want her to speak to anyone locally. She doesn't want to either. She buys new face cream and gives some to Alla.

One guy likes traffic-warden ladies and asks Clover to wear a skirt, roll up her sleeves to make her arms look muscular, and hit him.

'Are you embarrassed?' says one guy.

'No.'

Then he takes off his good imitation leg and has his arse licked.

A guy keeps staring and staring into her eyes. After she's seen the colour of his eyes long enough, it's very tedious. She avoids his gaze. One guy's sexiness comes through despite his unwashed nicotine smell. Clover ponders on that. Another has lips so thin they are almost nonexistent, as if to make up for an overgrown cock which he seems unable to manage. He says, 'I don't like to see you doing such a thing. Why don't you get a nice job in an office? It wouldn't pay so well, but it'd be better for you. Why don't you come with me to my cricket club one evening?'

Clover is amazed but doesn't show it. How could anyone want her to work in an office for her own good? How could anyone think she'd want to be seen with him outside this place?

One weekend she calls George, whom she knew before, and for a time she has black skin on her bed here. She looks at his hair, which has grown. Having sex with him she feels different, more active than she was. Then she notices herself slipping back into passivity when he does things the way he used to. Upstairs he's impressed by the stereo, which disappoints her.

Another weekend her friend Zeno comes round. He's a magician.

'It's sunny. What shall we do this afternoon?'

'Highgate Cemetery,' says Clover.

'Eh?'

'It's lovely,' says Clover.

And it pleases him as Clover thought it might. Hand in hand they run and skip through all the subtle English shades of grey. Stone and trees grow out of the ground together.

'I wish I'd brought my camera,' he says.

Clover is glad he hasn't. She only needs their eyes.

On Christmas Day, Clover enjoys the house alone. She watches colour telly and sips liqueurs from different pretty bottles that she finds in Harry's cupboard. She enjoys the telephone's silence. One call:

'Will you come out and visit me tomorrow? I'm at Richmond.'

Clover has never worked set times long enough for holidays to have a meaning for her.

'Yes, OK.'

And that's how she met Mr Purprick. He was thinnish, greyish, hairyish and wanted her to suck his purple prick. Sitting on his knee she ate chicken, the first meat for two years. She spent last Christmas with Tanzanians who were Hindus. He asked her where and how she worked and about Harry. He said Harry must be laughing all the way to the bank. Clover was laughing, so what did it matter if Harry was laughing too? He said he was a lawyer. He said police often raided massage parlours and checked all the dustbins for used Durex as evidence. Clover told him she was trying to get access to her children. She had once been illegally put into a mental hospital and thought that this frame-

up would be held against her. He said he would help
her. He would pay by cheque, but he'd mislaid his
chequebook. He would pay her the next time he saw
her. He said if anyone knew what she was doing she
stood no chance of seeing her kids.

The next day he phoned and said his chequebook
was definitely missing. Could Clover lend him some
cash till he got a new one? He might have to tell the
bank and go to the police, then he'd have to say she'd
been there and give them all the details.

New Year's Eve.

'Harry, I've an appointment at 9.30 in the morning
on New Year's Day, imagine that.'

'I bet he doesn't make it.'

'I hope so, if I get up that early.'

He makes it.

In the paper the next day, it says the comet Kohoutek
passes earth before departing into deep space, not to
return for hundreds of thousands of years.

Every night and sometimes when she's sitting on the
Dralon sofa and enjoying the place, Clover does self-
hypnosis and a small feeling of softness and peace
grows.

She applies for legal aid as Purprick advises. She
doesn't get an appointment, merely a form saying, 'You
have been refused legal aid.' But Mr Purprick will help
her do the case herself.

A busy afternoon of stroking, kneading, kissing,
caressing. Sighs and breaths. She feels her own breath.
After each client she washes and creams her hands and
tosses her hair. Upstairs she sits on the loo seat and
lights a cigarette. Harry's in the bath. She watches the
water ripple and darken his flesh.

'One said he was called Smith, the next one said he

was called Jones. Must be *Alias Smith and Jones* on the telly.'

They giggle. Smoke, steam and rippling water.

'I'm not keen on you having friends here. I get kinda nervous of people breaking in. When I was living in east London two guys broke in and ransacked the place. There wasn't anything for them to get but they knocked me out. I was concussed. I don't think I've really got over it. I don't have so much energy now, I get tired very easily. That's why I like to sell by phone as much as possible. I have to see customers every now and then, of course, but not too much, so it suits me fine.'

'Yeah,' said Clover. 'You know, I had an accident when I was twelve, thrown from a horse. I got concussion. I've been tired since then. It's funny, isn't it?'

It was worse than she said. From the age of ten she used to go horse riding with a friend every Saturday, just outside the town in Hampshire where they lived. She'd had seven falls with no harm. Seven were supposed to make you a rider. The eighth time she must have passed out as she was trotting along – colours appeared brighter and more glowing as they always did before she fainted, and the last thing she remembered was another friend riding towards her in the grey morning light looking as if she was wearing full evening make-up. They said the horse bolted and one of the gypsies living in the woods found her lying under a tree and got an ambulance. She awoke in hospital a couple of days later. They said she had a hairline fracture of the skull just above the neck on the right side, that her head must have hit the tree as she fell.

After that her body became weak – too weak to take part in sports or lead a normal life. Her voice was so weak it was almost a whisper; there was pain in her arms and shoulders when she walked. She couldn't cope with the cold and most of her body became numb in the English winter. She had cravings for food which she had to fight all the time. She knew her life couldn't begin till she had conquered this. When she ate she became hungrier and hungrier. She couldn't get used to that. She tried to control it. People punished her when they found her stuffing and starving.

Her face and body never stayed the same shape and size for more than a few months. She was frightened of being hit by things. She felt she became other people physically and got into their bodies but most of what she felt was their physical pain. Sex seemed the only thing that was good and safe.

Luckily, with all this suffering she was free of worries and emotional hurts. The future she hadn't thought of. Death always seemed near simply because she hadn't energy or money to last much longer, so she didn't feel deprived by not having possessions.

Even before the accident she was possibly slightly autistic and had a hearing problem – but no one knew, they still don't, nor does she. When she was three or four her mother wrote down the letters of the alphabet and the numbers for her, and each appeared to her in vivid colours, some in colours she'd never seen. Because of the colours she could read and spell perfectly at four. It gave her a natural memory system so her parents called her intelligent. She could read whole books without understanding the words. She still can't understand most medium-to-large words. Her friends called her slow.

Music was just noise to her. She had never known what a tune was, and used to look at people wonderingly when they listened to music. When she danced it was to people's bodies, not to the music. She couldn't distinguish accents or the direction of a sound or separate the different sounds of traffic or musical instruments. She took a while to hear what people said. She remembered people's words afterwards but didn't understand enough of them to reply. Her own voice was too soft to hear anyway.

She had always looked 'all right' to people, so they thought she was all right. This preserved her.

The kind of massage she does is not hard work. She has just enough energy for that, so having no social life suits her.

'Is this your earring?' Harry asks as he combs his circular bed.

'No.'

'Are you sure? Flavia's here this weekend. I've got to be careful.'

'It's not mine.'

Flavia, his girlfriend, works for some business in the West End. She talks about 'business' and 'at work' a lot. She worries about clothes and spends most of the weekend cleaning the house aggressively. She cooks meals for Harry, using a great deal of equipment. Clover looks at Flavia's long, old-looking hands.

'I don't know how you could,' she says to Clover.

Clover is happy sitting on the floor and watching *Robert's Robots* on television. Flavia and Harry talk about garages and getting petrol.

Monday morning at ten o'clock Harry brings Clover coffee in bed, which she likes. Upstairs, showered and dressed, they have more coffee. No sound from the phones yet. The news in stereo fills the lounge and kitchen. One-day train strikes, go-slow by ASLEF, heating restrictions, emergencies, regulations. Clover flicks through a book which Bondini left her. It's about pure foods and fasting. No coffee, tea, cigarettes or alcohol, only raw fruits and vegetables and grains, one day's fast every week. Clover wishes she could.

There is a large glass on top of the telly. Inside it green liquid mounts, fills, and blends into many shapes.

'I'm going round to my cousin's tonight. I don't get on well with her but she always cooks me a nice meal. That's really why I go. That's the best way to treat me, to spoil me,' Harry says. He smiles as he lounges on his thick carpet.

'Hmm,' says Clover. She thinks of Flavia cooking for him. Aila cooks for him and his cousin cooks for him. Harry brings her coffee first thing in the morning when she needs it most and she brings him coffee last thing at night when he likes it best. Clover never cooks for him. They have their own separate bits of food at separate times, of which Clover is glad. She has become secretive about eating.

A client rings up and asks Clover to meet him at the crossroads in the local shopping precinct. She stands there in her white fur coat. He doesn't appear. She looks at her reflection in the supermarket window. She feels conspicuous. Mr Purprick's stories of police checking dustbins for Durex go through her mind. And Mr Purprick knows how the press find things out, too. Has she been photographed? She enjoys the risk.

Back at Purple Petal Gardens.

'Hi! I'm Barnaby,' says the next client.

He's half black with a short bum and short hair. If his hair were longer he'd look blacker.

'I've a flat in the West End. It's really nice. Look, I'll

show it to you. I'll take less money than this guy here.
See what you think.'

He drives her for a long way into central London,
which is very dirty compared with Purple Petal Gardens. The flat is cold. The telephone makes a pleasant
sound.

'Yeah,' says Barnaby. 'I've muffled it with tissue
paper, else it'd drive you up the wall. See, it never
stops ringing. I've put cards all over London. What
d'you think?'

'Can I let you know?'

'Two weeks. Let me know in two weeks. I must get
someone in by then.'

Quite a lot of regulars turn up at Purple Petal Gardens, but there are always new ones and once-only
ones. So Clover never knows who will come each day.
She starts to look forward to tomorrow. She sits on the
Dralon sofa marvelling at the mounting and falling
patterns of green in the glass. She does self-hypnosis.
She feels peaceful inside.

Mr Purprick comes round. He says he hasn't found
his chequebook. He says he can't get money from his
other account. He must owe Clover for a massage and
borrow a few quid from her. She has to attend her
divorce hearing in three weeks. The access case might
be straight after it. In any case, she must be there to say
she wants access. Mr Purprick wants his three nipples
sucked. He tells of his friend on the *Daily Something*.

'He's been trying to do a story on you and this bloke.
He asked me about you, you know. I protected you. I
told him you were just doing it for a little while to get
the money together to go back to Australia with your
kids.'

Clover thinks that's a horrible story. She's not doing

it for her kids or to go back to Australia. She's doing it because it's the thing she wants to do. Her anger at the silly story grows and she contemplates his funny nipple structure.

He lies on the floor. 'Oh, shit on me. Pee on me,' he moans. 'Shit and pee in my mouth.'

She does. He whips out to the bathroom. She goes after him.

'Eh, you know, people often talk about things, say things, but they don't think of doing them.'

Clover can't imagine talking about something that you don't do. She says nothing.

'I'm going to try the diet in here,' says Harry, holding up Bondini's book on pure food. He stops drinking coffee. He fasts one day a week. Clover wishes she could. Aila had spent an afternoon preparing a Filipino meal for Harry, but Harry won't even taste it because it contains salt and the noodles aren't wholemeal. Clover eats it.

Next day, Clover skims her hands over fish-white backs, tastes sperm, coffee, washes her hands, brushes her teeth and tosses her hair.

The day after, she has flu. For three days she's in bed in pain. Music crashes through the ceiling. Her mind feels delirious. All her body is aching. Self-hypnosis can only soften her headache. She can't smoke. The phone sounds through the ceiling. Flavia is complaining:

'All that business lost, all that business lost.'

After four days the pain starts to ease. A client comes round to sell her an insurance policy. She's never had anything like that. She thinks, Why not? He shows her pictures of his kids in the garden and she notices his needing them. Zeno comes round with his brother.

Zeno is going to California. Clover has just enough strength to have sex with him.

Next morning Harry brings her strong coffee and a smile. The pain has gone.

'I won't have any more coffee or tea. I won't smoke again, either.'

She showers, goes upstairs and finds a peppermint tea bag. She drinks the clear green liquid and does self-hypnosis. She feels beautiful. A regular comes along. He's the only one she's had coffee with. After sex she goes upstairs, makes coffee for him and peppermint tea for herself. When she comes back, he and the money have gone through the window. She laughs and drinks peppermint tea.

Outside she buys a jar of pure unsweetened orange juice. It smells good. She shares it with Harry.

In the West End she buys a turquoise South Sea Island wraparound skirt. As he drapes it round her, the salesman paws her as close as possible to her cunt. Clover thinks it's funny – before she was a prostitute she would never notice such random touching. Now she does and she avoids it, drapes the skirt herself. She looks in the mirror, swirls the skirt, taking in all the fresh, new scents and smells of the store, and creates a bit of space for herself. She can choose and buy clothes instead of receiving ones that are given, swapped or found in dustbins.

The clients are there again so Flavia is less anxious. Clover can smell perfumes and aftershaves on the bus now. Her hands stroke clients' backs. She looks, strokes them and avoids their cigarettes.

'Oh, Dawn,' they say.

Zeno's brother comes round and takes her to the pub. She enjoys not smoking and sips a drink to keep him company, but she doesn't think she wants alcohol any more. She talks about Jesus Christ always being depicted blond and blue-eyed when he couldn't have been. Back at Purple Petal Gardens her neck chain falls off and Zeno's brother puts it on in a cliché-ridden way. Sex without a cigarette afterwards is so different, muses Clover.

In bed with Harry, she giggles at the antics of the day. Harry talks about petrol.

Clover sits in the kitchen, a towel round her washed hair. She looks at the strange naked wood.

'Clover!' Harry shrieks, running downstairs. 'It's happened. You've got to get out. I've just had a phone call. This guy – he said he's a reporter!'

'What?' Clover tucks her towel in more neatly.

'He said he knows I'm running a call-girl business and he wants to interview me. Oh, my God! That car outside. Are we being watched? We could be. You've got to get out today, and don't leave anything here.'

'It's OK, I'm going to court tomorrow but I'm staying with someone on the way tonight 'cos of the train go-slow. I better be sure I get there.'

Clover dries her hair. She kneels on the floor sorting through the books Bondini left her. She takes his notes on self-hypnosis and the pure-food book.

'Do you want a book on boats around Australia?'

'Thank you. I'm sorry to do this to you but I don't want any evidence left here.'

Clover phones some people where she hopes she can keep her suitcases. Harry says his mate will take them there. With a carrier bag, Clover sets off for Nigel's nudist camp.

'I'll miss seeing your boobs when we pass on the stairs.'

3
At Claude Catsilk's and a Regular Life

Lying in bed with Nigel, Clover wonders where she'll be tomorrow night. She remembers when she was last at Nigel's nudist camp. It was a breakaway nudist camp – not part of the organization to which nudist clubs are supposed to belong. She was serving ice cream. The top of the fridge was exactly level with her pubic hair. When she had to search for a special brand right at the bottom, she dived head over heels in, with the cool air on part of her and warm air on the rest of her. It was a nice feeling. Naked was the only way to work. She listens to Nigel's snore. It's like the sound of the sea. At the camp last time there was a group of three-year-olds sitting cross-legged, having a birthday party, and then a seventy-year-old ran up and started playing with them, and the three-year-olds didn't seem as young as the seventy-year-old. Inside the camp she was talked to by a guy with sloe-coloured eyes and hair. Later she saw him in clothes. She stopped desiring clothes after that.

Where can she go now? Barnaby Budge – he said she could use that flat. Where was it? She sees it in her mind's eye. After the court case she'll go back to London and look for it. She moves her arm away from Nigel, does self-hypnosis and sleeps.

In the courtroom she's full of smiles. Everyone else looks tense and anxious. She wonders why. Nodi, the guy she was married to, is twitching violently. Both in court and out he talks about 'our marriage being broken up'. Clover thinks it strange that he believes they were ever together. 'What are feelings?' she asked Nodi when she was seventeen, just before they were married. Her body was too cold and weak to have emotions yet. Married to Nodi it got even colder since in England they lived in a basement flat without heating. Only when they got to Australia did she start to feel.

She was closer to everyone else she had sex with during what he calls their marriage. But in reality she was only close to sex.

The access case is postponed to a later date. Good, she can get back to London to find Barnaby.

Nodi takes her to a pub to meet a middle-aged unhappy-looking guy and introduces her as 'the missus that was'. Clover remembers hearing that someone thought Nodi a repressed homosexual. She's never really considered Nodi. Perhaps he and the other guy both are. Nodi wants her address. She declines.

On the train she eats chocolate for breakfast, feeling guilty, and remembers the name Copplestone Mews. She makes a phone call. Harry's mate has delivered her cases and a story. They'll take her cases but not her. She finds Copplestone Mews near Marble Arch. It's dark but one house has lights on. She knocks on the door and a girl who calls herself Gemma answers.

'Barnaby? Is Barnaby here?'

Gemma says he isn't. But he'll be along soon.

The flat is warmer now. They drink herb tea together. Gemma is into health foods, but she doesn't look very healthy. She smokes long cigarettes. Barnaby comes in wearing a striped gold suit tight over his short bum.

'Yeah, sure you can work here. There's so much business, we need two girls.'

He takes Clover out to a fish-and-chip restaurant.

'Gemma won't be here much longer. I wanna get something started, make a kill and get out, that's the only way. Then maybe I can get something lined up in the States, San Francisco. I think you might be the girl. We could make a fortune out there. You'd be driving round in a Cadillac.'

'I don't want a Cadillac,' says Clover.

'Well, any car you want you could have if you play your cards right.'

Clover doesn't want a car, but San Francisco she wouldn't mind.

'You can stay at Copplestone till you find a place. But all your gear goes in the cupboard in the corridor. It mustn't look as if you live here.'

Over the meal of fish and chips, which Clover does not want though she doesn't say so, Barnaby says:

'If you move in with someone, don't tell him or any boyfriend that you work in a massage parlour. Just say you work as a secretary.'

Clover knows she's not going to pretend any such thing.

'And always put your money straight in the bank.'

She feels his relaxing black smell as she has sex with him. It looks as if he won't be staying the night. She smiles, looking forward to being cosy and peaceful by herself.

It's a two-room flat. Each room has a massage table in it. One room has a divan which Clover sleeps on, the other has a basin and shower. In the passage there's a loo and a cupboard for Clover's things.

Next day the phone rings and rings. Barnaby is putting green carpet down. He seems to have advertised a lot.

'I saw your ad in Fulham.'

'I saw your ad in Richmond.'
'I saw your ad in Notting Hill.'
'I saw your ad in Maida Vale.'
'I saw your ad in Kilburn High Road.'
'I saw your ad in King's Road.'
'I saw your ad in Balham.'
'I saw your ad in West End Lane.'
'I saw your ad in Shepherd's Bush.'
'I saw your ad in Baker Street.'
'I saw your ad in Piccadilly.'
'I saw your ad in Bayswater.'

'Gemma's not here today. Put the money in the Yellow Pages. I'll be here to collect it. By the way, try and get them to have a shower first, otherwise the place'll stink. English people, they're filthy.'

'I know.'

'Keep the window open. That helps.'

Most of the guys who turn up are from the strange grey world of offices. Their white bodies, greyish with city grime, have asymmetrical genitals, torn-looking balls, pains in their lower back from too much time in cars. Clover is amazed that they don't shower. They soap and dry about a third of their body. Talcum powder on wet hairy legs, the hair often much darker than the skin. The subtle, grubby English middle-class smell. She remembers when she was in Notting Hill in cheap, clean, ironed clothes and saw people who wore nice, expensive clothes, but were filthy. Once they are powdered, on the table, she massages them as little as possible. They turn over, pull their hands through her wraparound skirt, through her pants, through her breasts. They talk about themselves and the weather.

Her nipples are rigid with cold. She was not made for this climate. On Shellweather Beach in Australia, with

Bill and Ben, her kids, and some neighbours, her body felt comfortable for the first time since the accident. The feel of smooth rocks under her feet, the coarse white sand blending with coconut oil under her fingernails.

'Does it turn you on?'

'Do you like this?'

'What else turns you on?'

'Yes, do that, but very easy, very slow, I don't want to come just yet. Oh, careful, I nearly came then.'

'Oh, I came so soon then, I don't usually. It must be because it's the first time with you. Yes, that must be it.'

'I don't know why I'm like this. I've never taken so long. It must be because it's the first time with you. I feel nervous. I don't really know you. Where do you come from?'

Eh? thinks Clover.

Some just roll over and come quietly. She doesn't have to say anything and her thoughts wander freely.

She's having sex on the massage table. Barnaby's in the other room. She has to pretend there's no one in the other room or the guy'll be scared. She doesn't like Barnaby being around when she's working.

One guy looks like a tramp, but he's spotlessly clean. He's only got enough for a straight massage. Later he comes back with two and a half times what Clover asks, in clean new notes.

'Do you like being massaged?'

'Mm,' says Clover.

She lays her showered body on the table and he powders her delicately all over, massages and kisses her tummy sweetly. He especially powders and kisses her feet. She smiles and wonders if he pinched the money. Perhaps he's been followed here, she thinks as she wanks him.

Someone comes, but nothing comes.

'I've had a vasectomy. It's quite normal.'

'Oh.'

One guy, a professional gambler, comes regularly. He is one of the few who look just as much themselves without clothes. He and Clover manoeuvre themselves into the acrobatic field of sex on the massage table.

'I've plans for a club, something different, in Shepherd's Bush,' says Barnaby. He only comes round once a day now to collect what Clover and Gemma leave him in the Yellow Pages. So Clover sits in front of the fire with Gemma, answering the phone, chatting, drinking herb tea, eating too much, reading astrological and fucking magazines that are lying around.

Sometimes it's too cold to use the loo in the hall. Clover pees in the wash basin and nearly falls off the wall with it. Barnaby wonders why when he mends it. Clover thinks of finding somewhere to live. Barnaby fakes some references for her. The thought of a cool, gentle black guy in blue denim comes into her mind. She goes to Finsbury Park to look at a place. She gets no reply. Well, she's lived in Finsbury Park before. She doesn't want to live anywhere a second time.

'Hi, Clover, hello, you look lovely,' says a round Nigerian guy. 'Ibrahim, he's been looking for you. You went to Kent. Where did you go then? We couldn't find you. Why did you leave?'

'A few places.' Clover smiles. Finsbury Park was only a few months ago but it seems a long time.

'Your phone number, he must get in touch with you. Look, you can get me at this number. I'm going back to Nigeria soon. You must come to my party.'

'I'll try.'

'And Ibrahim, he misses you.'

'I'll be in touch.'

She eludes him and runs into Finsbury Park tube station. The cool black guy in the blue denim who had appeared in her mind appears on the station platform.

'Hi. I can feel these strong vibrations coming from you.'

'Oh,' says Clover.

A train arrives and they get on. When he asks her she says, 'I work in a massage parlour.' She enjoys the novelty of telling someone she has a job and most of all a job she wants to do, a job she has no dislike for. She smiles as Claude talks to her and questions her.

'Meet me after work.'

Clover is silent.

'Don't just say so if you're not going to. Take a chance. There are so many chances lost in life.'

'OK.'

At Copplestone Mews she screws a hunky, cheese-coloured guy as quickly as possible, then she can shower so she's ready for Claude Catsilk.

'He has such a poetic face,' says Clover as they watch a Bruce Lee film.

Claude is fresh out of prison. His flat is cold and cavernous. He's putting basic white all over it which makes it look stark and even colder. They huddle on a stumpy sofa in front of a fuzzy TV picture. He says Clover can stay there if she needs an address for the court case. Then he stands on his head and Clover wishes she could do that. His arms look friendly and curvaceous, his profile is bold but he looks sad from waist to ankles with stretch marks or scars across his buttocks. His feet always look happy and comfortable.

Clover easily projects herself into the best bits of people's bodies. She chooses the feet of Claude.

In the freezing bedroom, Claude dictates how the sheets and blankets are to be made up skin-tight on the mattress to keep out the cold. They can hardly get in. They have sex jammed tight.

'Have you been with black men before?'

'Yes.'

'It smells of sex in here,' says Claude, sniffing in the morning.

They run themselves lovely long baths out of a gas geyser. Claude has taken the cover off and the grey intricacies of its insides stand out against the portion of grey brick wall which Claude has left bare.

'It's lovely,' says Clover. 'They really go together.'

'Hmm. Interesting that you noticed that.'

Later. 'You read *Time Out*. Would you call yourself a radical, then?'

'No,' says Clover.

She isn't quite sure what a radical means, but she wouldn't call herself anything.

On Monday Clover goes in to work. A heavy-sounding lady rings up.

'Someone from your establishment has been putting your ads over mine. You'd better cool it 'cos I know some very dodgy people. OK?'

'OK. I don't know anything about it but I'll pass your message on. What's your card?'

'Drama lessons by Lulu. Bye-bye.'

'She's cool, really cool,' says Barnaby, twinkling his eyes. 'Such a scene she's got there. Dope, it's beautiful, you can just smoke.'

Clover thinks that a waste of time.

'I better check what she's had done to my cards.' He grins.

The day is quiet, and over red herbal tea Gemma tells her story.

'Ze first time I 'ad sex eet was een an hotel een Eetaly, I was fifteen, but I was still a virgin afterward. And ze guys dey respected me for zat. Dey paid me to do ozzer t'ings.'

She talks on and on. She talks as if men and money are inseparable.

'My husband 'e was a terrible man. 'E hurt me so much.'

Clover hasn't felt hurt by anyone. She just feels the pain of others. Gemma has been working in massage parlours for six years, yet after three months Clover has as much money as Gemma, whose catch phrase is 'I needa da monee'. She often says, 'So-and-so 'e came to visit me. 'E eez an old friend. 'E give me twenty pound 'cos I needa da monee. Dees man, dees friend of mine, 'e visit me so I 'and 'im my rent book, I ask for a month's rent. I mean, 'e not offer me marriage, so 'e should pay ze rent.'

In the other room, Clover is gently kissed by a guy and feels glad that she's not Gemma.

Then a guy back from abroad, with interesting stories and a nice clean tan, who doesn't agitate about money.

It's the second time she's taken a taxi. She taxies back to Claude's with her gear. He wears a white kerchief round his face as protection against dust when he works on the wall. Clover buys fruit juice for him, and puts money in the gas and electricity meters. She feels a happy power to keep herself and him warm.

'It looks like a railway station in here. You must put them all away.'

So most of her bags go in a cupboard she finds.

In the bathroom with the exposed geyser and bare bit of wall, Claude lies in the steaming bath. Clover sits on the loo seat writing to Prince. She can send him money. You need it more inside than outside. In reply to his question she tells Claude whom she is writing to.

'You have my loyal support,' he says. 'I was in prison, not for murder or anything. It was my university of life.' He smiles at the bathwater and steam.

'I was put into a mental hospital. That was my university of life. Prisons, mental hospitals, they're all the same,' says Clover.

'No, it's not true,' he says and cuts her story. 'Where I was, these seven officers came to get me out of my cell. They started kicking me in the balls, yelling "Nigger, nigger" – you know, I know karate so I can defend myself.' He demonstrates his right thigh defending his balls, splashing the water. 'But seven?' He smiles. 'They were obeying their orders.'

Clover soaps Claude's back with a gossamer touch.

'Rub me harder.'

But Clover can't. She can feel the pain in his balls where she has no balls and pain all over his body.

On the plane to London, repatriated from Australia against her will, every now and then she seemed to see little bits of beach go past the plane window. She thanked her lucky stars she'd known not to take the drugs they gave out in the convict-built day centre in Sydney. She was being sent to her parents, who now lived in London. She'd never been there. She knew no one in England except Nodi and their two children, who lived with his parents somewhere else she'd never been. Nodi had known none of her addresses since she left him two years before, and didn't know she was leaving Australia. Lucky, since he probably still wanted to kill her.

In England there were no colours, people thought she was strange because she bathed every day, and the men seemed like coathangers wearing suits. Her parents wanted nothing to do with her. Four policemen came to take her away. 'Who were those people?' asked the police after they had put her in an ambulance. She didn't know where they were going, but she saw the police didn't like what they were doing. They drove through unknown grey to the sign HOVER HOSPITAL. 'Will you be all right here?' She said yes to reassure them. It felt as if they didn't want to leave her there. She didn't know where she was or how she had been put there, or if she could ever get out. On the pretext of offering her a bath they took away her clothes and the key to her parents' house. She had no money and no friends on the outside. With Jed she formed the nearest to marriage so far, a bond. He was a trusty there. Staff were less threatening when they knew she was with him.

'I want to observe what your tastes are,' says Claude.

She hides from him the fact that she doesn't know how to put a cassette in the cassette player. At night she lies in bed thinking she doesn't have any tastes. She looks at the soft pigskin suitcase and sharp hats on Claude's wardrobe from the moneyed days of dealing. She does self-hypnosis and sleeps.

There will be a visit from a social worker before the court case. Clover phones Mr Purprick for advice on what to say to a social worker.

'Why didn't you tell me you'd left that place? You should have asked me for help.'

He comes round to Copplestone Mews.

'What sort of guy runs this place?'

'Why do you have to know that?'

'I must know these things if I'm to protect you. Is he coloured?'

'No, he's not.'

She doesn't give him her address at Claude Catsilk's.

'I was talking to a barrister about your case. He thinks it a very good idea that you represent yourself with me to advise you.'

He has his three nipples played with. He still can't pay Clover what he owes her. He has bills.

'You need an affidavit.' He starts to compose one. 'You'll soon get used to being Mum again.'

Clover never was and has no intention of being 'Mum'. She thinks of how many extra nipples there seem to be among the clients at this place. Some days are a sort of spot-the-nipple contest.

A public-school guy who asks her to beat him. She is wearing a leather belt which suits him fine. Fortunately for Clover, he is happy about the pain.

A white South African who says how traumatic it is to share public transport with Jamaicans and how the blacks back home are not ready for civilization yet, although the whites do what they can to help them. Clover strokes. A guy with war wounds, great chunks of his flesh cut out long ago.

'Which war?' Clover politely enquires. The wounded parts are much warmer than the rest of his body. Clover is fascinated. He wants her to pull his head sharply out from his neck so that it clicks.

'It's all right, it's quite safe. I used to go to a chap

who did it for me but he's dead now.' Click. 'Ah, that's better. Thank you, dear.'

Cup of tea with Gemma.

'I'm going out weet' dis guy, 'e's come 'ere often. 'E eez really nice.'

When he arrives Clover can't imagine wanting to go out with him.

A large guy who has a Heath-like laugh when he comes. He offers to get a flat for Clover. He won't mind what she does there as long as she's free when he wants to visit her, and he gets to choose her wardrobe. Clover doesn't want anything like that and avoids it by saying neither yes nor no. To be available to someone like that!

Barnaby arrives and they have sex in the nicely warmed-up room. He's off to Barbados where his father's been burned in a fire and is dying. He's going to check out San Francisco afterwards, see a guy there. Clover feels his father's burns. They kiss goodbye. She goes to the waste bin to find a jar of jam that Gemma has chucked out after one teaspoonful. It is pure fruit and sugar, no preservatives, from a very expensive health-food shop that Gemma frequents. Clover rinses it. She finds a beautiful piece of black velvet in the dustbin outside. On the tube back she tries not to feel Barnaby's father's pains. Round Westbourne Park the tower blocks, flyovers and lights from buildings, cars and streets make changing patterns in the slow dusk. 'Work, sleep, tube – how much more can you take?' says the graffiti.

She shows Claude a little biro sketch she's made of his profile. It has no eyes. 'What is your motive for interrupting me watching the telly?' T. Dan Smith is on. Claude likes the jam, but doesn't like the velvet having come from the dustbin. Clover asks him how much the rent is.

'Yes, I was gonna mention that.' She pays him half.

In the cold corridor she holds carpet for him to cut with a razor blade. He suddenly hugs her. He brushes his teeth long and loud every day and tells Clover the right place to put the toothbrush. He turns the radio on at seven in the morning when he's doing a decorating job. When he's doing deals he comes in late at night and makes a noise with his clothes. Clover has never had such a regular life. She watches him chomping muesli, little white flecks of it on his skin.

'You look like a horse,' she says.

'You implying I eat noisily?'

'No, it's nice.'

Claude does a headstand, his body ultrablack against the wall he's made white. Gravity brings his soft cock to a surreal erection. Clover looks at it and thinks about the court case and wonders what will happen.

In bed he reads the *Evening Standard*.

'It's about shops in Hampstead. More and more are turning into boutiques and hi-fi shops. Hardware shops, grocers and things like that are decreasing at an amazing rate.'

'How interesting.' Clover doesn't understand the significance. Most shops contain things she hasn't thought of having.

Another night Clover is looking at Claude. He is asking her for money, to set up a deal, but he doesn't ask her straight as a friend. She guesses Gemma might ask her 'friends' for money in the same way. She gives it to him.

She phones Harry from Copplestone Mews.

'That was a nasty joke to play,' he says.

'Eh?'

'Your friend phoned. He said that you'd got him to pretend to be a reporter when he rang before. How could you?'

'No, I never, honestly!' Thinking, why would I do that? 'I wonder who it was.'

Harry brings mail around next morning. A letter from Prince with a colour photo in it, taken in his cell with his high-school certificates on the wall behind him. A card from Anon, saying, 'I've found I have an infection. I thought I should let you know.'

She and Harry kiss on the bed. She finds the nearest special clinic. It's called Martha Mary. She wonders why. She has a minor infection, nothing serious. At work, Gemma talks about her last two nose jobs and how she's planning a third and ultimate one, except that there's not much left to operate on.

Clover stands by the massage table working away and thinking her own thoughts. Bondini says most illnesses are psychosomatic. Suddenly, she notices the guy's feet. All ten toes are webbed, like a duck's. It's like something out of a horror movie. She looks at his face. So is that. She imagines the film – the girl victim is trying to crawl out of a churning, oozing, muddy hole, her delicate white hands are vainly trying to reach firm ground, her breasts are nearly out of her tattered garment. Then, suddenly, she sees these ten gigantic webbed toes. She screams and falls helplessly into the oozing mud.

'You look so happy,' he says.

At lunchtime, Clover and Gemma walk among the ancient, massive, grey buildings and black statues of central London. Clover feels oppressed by them. She tries not to notice them, but she can't bear the ugliness of buildings, especially old ones. They go into a vegetarian restaurant. There are corn sheaves on the walls. Wholemeal bread, grains, all types of legumes, multicoloured salads in silver-coloured bowls. Clover has a salad and likes being able to eat something beautiful for a change. Gemma has sweet coffee and wine and smokes. Gemma is talking about conning one of her 'old friends' into letting her have a £400 deposit so she can move into a posher flat. She talks about the two of them setting up in a flat, charging double the money and not having to give it to anyone. Clover listens. She wants to do that herself, by herself, to answer her own phone. She leaves Gemma going to meet this 'old friend'.

Back at Copplestone Mews, Mr Purprick arrives. He needs money to decorate his house. He tells Clover that a friend of his has been here and was ripped off by the other girl, and is thinking of making a complaint to the council.

The guy with the Heath-like laugh asks again about setting her up in a flat.

A guy with a job in jewellery wants Clover to work in hotels.

'You look innocent enough,' he says. 'They'd let you in.'

Clover just says, 'Hmm.' She thinks of Claude doing his headstand as part of his yoga and wishes she could.

She showers and returns to Claude's.

When she opens her mouth to tell him about her infection, he puts his finger on her lips and forbids her to say anything. Later, *The Loves of Napoleon* is on the telly. Napoleon is exploding on account of one of them. 'Wow! Incredible to lose one's cool like that!' says Claude.

At one in the morning Clover tells him and he explodes like Napoleon. Clover cries. The infection is clear in a week. Spring light comes slowly but Claude is cool. Clover buys an economy pack of rubbers and spends time on the massage table with the gambler.

A luxurious garden and swimming pool on telly. 'The sort of life style you had in Australia, I guess,' Claude says, accusingly.

Eh? thinks Clover. 'You can't live on thin air,' said a nun at the hostel she was sent to by the day-care centre in Sydney. Clover was surprised because she'd lived on quite a lot of it. Claude's fart becomes more aggressive. Claude creates a character with her name to attack.

Clover buys Vim.

'You're materialistic, all these things you buy.'

Claude flatters her for more money. She believes she should give him the benefit of the doubt. Clover wants to leave but thinks it would be good for her character to stay in one place for a while, so she stays. She buys another sleeping bag so they can sleep in a double sleeping bag on the two single mattresses.

One Saturday morning, Claude says, 'Every morning we must lift the mattresses, unzip the sleeping bags and put them underneath. Then, just the coverlet on top. Come on, now.'

'That's stupid,' says Clover.

'Come on, now, that's the right way.'

'No, you can if you like, but I won't.'

'Huh huh huh huh.'

She throws a hairbrush. He lies down and does meditation. She catches a friendly double-decker bus and goes round London on it. She feels different.

It is spring. For the first time she lets herself begin to like the English spring. She lets herself notice little buds popping up here and there. She looks at the huge ancient buildings and black stone of the statues and feels less weighed down by them. She goes to the restaurant Gemma showed her, eats and relaxes. She looks at the people. She loves their faces and bodies and feels herself become them for a while.

She visits Bondini's mate Roland and has sex on his carpet. He offers her a king-size Virginia cigarette – 'You don't smoke now?' He sucks garlic capsules for his health. Roland is leaving the flat soon. She asks if he can fix it so that she can take it on after him; he says he'll try.

'Why don't you get a nice live-in job with a family?' he says.

Clover gasps inwardly. Of course, he doesn't know of her good luck, of what has happened in the last four months.

'I'll be in touch,' she says, 'about the flat.'

Claude and Clover go to see *La Grande Bouffe*. The film is about some middle-class Frenchmen who go to a large country mansion to eat themselves to death. Clover cries throughout and on the way back. She confesses to Claude that when she starts eating she can't stop. She even eats things she doesn't like. She buys food in secret and eats frantically when no one is looking. Claude starts to spy on her.

'Yeah, I caught you that time, didn't I?' He starts checking the waste bins to see what she's eaten, and smelling the toilet. His look is that of a mental-hospital nurse or prison officer. It says, 'Either way you're guilty.'

He tells her again where to put the toothpaste and how to light matches. He says a woman police officer has been following him. 'Don't let the neighbours in.'

One day, Clover is sitting on the loo and he says, 'I love you.' She guesses he's timed it for that.

'You see how they were looking at us on the tube?'

Clover is always being looked at when she's with a guy, so she never notices it.

'If what you do is right, why don't you just do it and be an example to me instead of telling me all the time?'

'I dig, I dig.' But he doesn't.

In bed, she says, 'It's wrong to treat people like specimens to pick up and observe.'

'You think I'm mixed up? Do you?'

Barnaby is back. They kiss, laugh, tell jokes. She notices how her voice sounds happier at work. She can laugh there.

Claude complains that her clothes aren't smart. He fasts and Clover wishes she could.

'Sometimes I fast except for pure white rice. It's amazing. My shit turns white.'

'Oh,' says Clover from her bath.

He brushes his teeth and decides on the right place for her to put the toothpaste.

Ollie comes round; he was in 'Her Majesty's holiday camp' with Claude. They drink a rare bottle of sherry. Claude is surprised to learn that Clover has had sex with men and girls together. Ollie talks about his girlfriend who's working at a massage parlour. She prefers it not to be known that she pulls plonkers in Soho, because her sister is a famous singer.

Claude says, 'Oh. Do *you* pull plonkers, then?'

Clover is amazed. Surely he knows what goes on. 'Yes, of course.'

'Do you sometimes get carried away? Oh no, I won't embarrass you.'

She notices how sad his laugh often is as he talks to Ollie.

Suddenly Claude says, 'Do you believe in God, then?'

'Yes.'

He laughs accusingly.

'The yoga you do, the self-hypnosis I do, and God – they're all part of the same thing,' she says.

'No, they're not.' He closes like a prison gate.

'They're just different shades of the spectrum,' she says, curving her hand in an arc and looking at Ollie. 'All part of the same thing, like a rainbow.'

Next day, Clover goes to Mr Purprick's house for advice about the social worker whose visit is imminent. Mr Purprick lies on the floor with his highly coloured one and three nipples. He doesn't tell her much.

When she sees Claude again, she's Out with a big O.

'Why?' she says. 'Why are you throwing me out? What's the real reason?' and she cries all over the garden.

'The social worker's coming on Monday, isn't she? You can stay till then. Then, if you're not out I'll throw your stuff on the pavement. I would. I've nothing to lose.'

In bed he wants to have sex and she doesn't. She knows he wants to because he has to protect his 'cool' image. Her life is civilized now, peaceful compared to what it used to be. She floats on self-hypnosis.

In the early morning she takes a walk and spends the day in bed with a guy a few streets away. She tells him nothing of herself, and enjoys the spring sun on his bed.

In the evening she has a bath and takes the tube to Brixton to see John and Sue – she shared the flat in Finsbury Park with them last year. Walking along

Brixton platform, feeling her hessian bag on her shoulder, she thinks, Yes, this is me moving, but now I have some money it's not frightening to move.

Going up the escalator, two guys try to pick her up. She feels the game of chance and wonders who it'll happen to be. Eric says he's from Guyana, a telephone operator. She gives him the phone number of where she's going.

John and Sue say they live in Stockwell so Clover guesses it's really Brixton. She sits watching telly with them. Sue is from Zambia and John from Southend. They work in offices and worship planes and flying. They are self-conscious about living together and scared their parents will make a sudden swoop on them. John puts his arm around Sue and nearly touches her nipple.

'Don't, you'll make Clover embarrassed,' she says.

Every weekday evening they tell everything that's happened to them.

Clover thinks how Claude would condemn their untidiness and everything else about them, and vice versa. She looks at Sue's beautiful feet and legs coated by city grime and bruised and crushed by city shoes and pavements. Cleaned, oiled and massaged, they would be angelic.

'You've got really nice legs.'

John looks embarrassed.

4

Brixton, Tooting and Peachy Hill

'You live in a fantasy world,' says the social worker. Clover has just told her she's been thrown out. The social worker talks of 'facing up to reality'. She doesn't look at all real and Clover wonders if she has a world.

'Why are you doing this?' she asks Claude.

'Because you're a liar.'

'What have I lied about?'

'Head pest. You've got head pest.'

'But nettles in hair conditioner have nothing to do with head pest!'

He blames her for having some money. He blames her for buying things for him. He wants money for buying and selling. He can't bear her to take some of the things from the flat and watches her like a jailer. Soon she's off in a taxi, her tears drying. Her things go in a cupboard under the stairs which John has cleared out.

In the evening she visits Eric. He introduces her to his cock, which is called Abdul. She hasn't met one called Abdul before.

Next day, from a part of London she lived in before and won't again, she sends Claude some postal orders. The postmark will put him off her scent. As she's getting off the tube near Copplestone Mews a guy asks her for money.

'Don't be frightened,' he says.

She's not. She's holding three carrier bags, her jeans have popped open. She's discreetly gyrating her hips to keep her jeans up and trying to get money out of her purse with no hands to spare. She manages, then gets in to work. She relaxes with self-hypnosis and smiles.

A client is really turned on by having Durex put on him gently and slowly. Clover puts two of hers on. Then he puts his special one on. It has bumps on it. She thinks maybe he likes rubbers better than his own cock. They have a little natter about it.

A slender guy with no obtrusive muscles, son of a kung fu master.

'We had to do it every evening, like homework.'

Her hands glide over him and she marvels at what this body must be able to do.

In the street Clover sees a little black kitten with a white tuft on its forehead. At Roland's she meets Mr Kitten. He is large and black with a big head and a sweet little white tuft in front. He works at Heathrow where he spends his time sleeping in a cupboard. For them Clover does straight massage.

Roland is talking jokingly about Bondini's self-hypnosis sessions. 'He had groups of people lying down on this floor. Crazy!' There are drinks, which Clover doesn't have. Roland tells a story of Bondini in Singapore. He'd taken up with a girlfriend and had then discovered she was a call girl. He went and smashed up her and her flat. Clover remembers sitting between Bondini and Roland in the far-off days of five months ago. Bondini was saying women's liberationists were really lesbian and Roland was not disagreeing. Clover had flicked through Germaine Greer and *History of Nigeria* and *Victorian Underworld* simultaneously while waiting for a modelling session at an art school. She nearly spoke. But she was grateful to Bondini because he had taught her self-hypnosis, whatever else he might have done. Roland's landlord already has future tenants.

At Mr Kitten's, in a high-rise council flat in Wembley for the weekend. He won't let her go to the loo without his dressing gown on. He's worried that she won't eat chicken so she does. Soppy music plays. At least, the words are soppy. She can't feel the music. 'A woman like you should never be alone. I wanna help. I wanna help. I wanna help.' Why should the poor woman not be alone if she wants? And why should she want him to help her? And could he help her anyway?

At Copplestone the Heath-like laugh is louder and still wants to set her up in a flat.

She visits Mr Purprick for the last time. An appointment with another social worker is looming.

Can you come here with a black guy? I want to see him fucking you all over the house. You mustn't tell him there's anyone here. You must have a friend. I'll just hide in a cupboard. I've managed to persuade my friend not to make a complaint about Copplestone Mews – for a while anyway. I just want to watch you being fucked by a big black guy. And one more thing – just as a favour for an old friend. What time do you get to work?'

'Twelve noon.'

'Ring me when your first customer arrives, leave the phone off the hook, then I can hear you at it.'

She never goes back to Copplestone Mews. Next day she rests on the sofa at John and Sue's.

At a flat agency in Kensington High Street she applies for a flat, using Barnaby's fake references. She just hopes they won't check them. She's nervous. She's never been in a place like this.

At John and Sue's she does self-hypnosis before they

come back. She comes to the bit where she gets in a peaceful scene from nature. Regularly as clockwork her beloved beach appears and she lies on the clean coarse sand among smooth ancient rocks all open to the sky. This time the beach is so blurred it's hardly there. And she can't get to what there is of it because of a huge black barrier. What has happened to the beach, to her?

She takes the last tube to Tooting, where Eric has finished his night shift at the telephone exchange. Cuddle on the sofa.

'I'm gonna shed my skin like a snake,' she says. He thinks she's referring to marriage and divorce, but she's not. He talks of his ex-marriage as if not being married is worse than being married. Clover is silent. It's something that has never touched her. She tells him of the first guy she loved – the first black guy she knew, in Sydney.

One client at Copplestone has given her his phone number. A client for when she has her own place to work. She visits him in Streatham and gives him a massage. But she has to breathe his cigarette smoke and whisky fumes and watch telly with him and the money is given to her haphazardly, some time at the end of the proceeding. She's not sure where to put it. At Copplestone and Purple Petal Gardens the money was handed over first and put in a certain place to mark the beginning of a ritual. Here not much of the time is spent on fucking. It's neither one thing nor the other.

Mr Kitten tells her he has got an infection from her. In John and Sue's kitchen they drink black coffee. He says, 'One day, if you meet a Mr Right, everything will be all right.' She doesn't know what to say. She's annoyed at his stupid remark.

She's been too long at John and Sue's. She takes two

polythene bags and goes on to deepest south Croydon. She cuddles Jed, her former bin mate who is staying on a mattress on the floor of his sister's bedsit. She sinks deep into his dark eyes. When he was seventeen his mother died and his first girlfriend split. Since then doctors have been telling him he was sick. They filled him with so many drugs that he believed them, became addicted to their drugs.

In Hover Hospital she had seen people foaming at the mouth and turning green, and nearly all the inmates had the shakes from drugs. Clover got the shakes in sympathy. The two months she was there could have been for ever, she never knew if or when they'd let her out; she had no money, didn't know by what law she was put there, and knew no one outside except her parents. It was touch and go if you were put on Section indefinitely and sent to wards which no one left, where patients were locked in chairs during the day, and given one slice of Spam for their meal. The last four weeks, a particular nurse came round, on her night duty, flashing a torch on Clover and threatening to move her to one of those.

Clover and Jed created their own environment in the cloakroom of Jed's ward. It was the very best ward, patients were allowed to make cups of tea. Jed's beautiful cups of tea, No. 10 cigarettes and Jim Reeves on a tiny record player. With Jed, Clover started to find out how the place operated, and she tried to get through to him and other friends not to take the drugs and not to believe it when they were told they were sick.

She didn't know why they let her out to a hostel for discharged mental patients, with no heating and full of former patients with the shakes. She got out of that to London, the nearest place. No one knew she existed, she hoped. Inside herself she felt stronger now, she had learned so much through being with Jed. She knew for the first time that she had some strength. People on the outside thought those inside were sick, people on the inside thought they were sick too. She wasn't in either place. Still scared that the police could put her back inside again, she told no one. She moved nineteen times the first year in London. She went through law books in public libraries, and found she should have been seen by at least two doctors before she was taken away.

When Clover was with Jed she could overcome his brainwashing for a while. Wherever she went he would always be with her in some way, even if she never saw him again. That was the way she loved him.

'I been offered six grand to do a prison sentence for someone,' he tells her. 'I mean, I done the bin so many times, prison'd be a walkover. The only thing that bothers me is that I got a prison record as well as a mental-hospital one. It'll ruin my prospects.'

'D'you have any prospects?'

She stays there three nights. Talks with his sister about honey. There's no bathroom there. She baths at John and Sue's, and arrives at the social worker's office.

He looks at her in her long pink dress and black jacket.

'I can't conceive of you as a mother,' he says. 'You don't look like a mother. The stepmother is big and middle-aged and busty and looks like a mother.'

'Oh.' Clover nearly gets the giggles. She's never met anyone who didn't think she was busty. From the age of three she looked older than she was. At fourteen she looked about twenty. Then, at eighteen, when her first child was born, people suddenly started thinking she looked younger, but still busty. He doesn't tell her much about what might happen or when the case will be. Then he talks about the painting on his office wall and how he's got to collect a woman alcoholic from one prison and take her to another. Clover wonders how he can see beauty in paintings yet put a woman in prison.

She soaks and soaks in another bath, showers herself all over, feels soft and comfortable like a mass of flower petals.

At Victoria she phones a racing driver who might let her have a flat to share. He's out. She phones the agency and looks at a pair of curvaceous but slightly dry hands in the next booth. No luck from the agency. She focuses on the hands. The eyes belonging to the hands look at her. She and the guy leave their phone booths.

'How much is it to phone Brighton?'

'I don't know.'

'What are you doing?'

'Looking for a place to live.'

'I just happen to have a vacant room.'

'Where?'

'Peachy Hill.'

'Where's that?'

'I'll show you.'

They get into the car, which is peachy-coloured.

'What work do you do?'

'Massage.'

He looks at her and knows what she means, which pleases her.

'Ah, yes. These Maltese boys, they say, "Thwack, thwack, where's the mahnee?" You mean you ain't working today?'

Clover giggles politely.

'Ah, you know what I mean.'

Then he goes on about marriage and divorce for a while, so Clover starts to look out of the window and wonders where Peachy Hill is.

The car stops somewhere in north London. The house is pale strawberry. The address is number 3 Peachy Rise. They go through a multicoloured glass door, then through another. Cyrrhus opens a third door and there it is – the magic room.

'Will you be using it for business?'

Clover thinks it best to say Yes.

5

The Magic Room

'That was a fantastic gobble, like a French girl.'

What you might call a nonreturnable deposit, thinks Clover, smiling to herself. In exchange for most of the notes she has on her, she gets a key and an old rent book with the name Patel on it.

At Jed's she tells him the good news. His mate's there, a mental-hospital nurse. Clover sits in the back of the car on the way to Stockwell and is nearly buried in their cigarette smoke. The guy is telling Jed that he spends most of his working day hitting people for masturbating. Jed sits there suffering. Goodbye again to him and she'll ring him when the phone's on. A few things from John and Sue's and she'll ring when the phone's on and pick up the rest.

She takes a long tube journey across London to the place she never knew existed. At the station before Clover's the train stops and doesn't start again. The passengers get out. There's a crowd at one end of the platform. The driver has dropped dead. What a place to die. She walks in the warm dark evening to Peachy Rise and through the two coloured glass doors. The room is quiet, white, gentle. No one knows she's here. It's beautiful. She sleeps for fifteen hours.

A tap at the door. It's Cyrrhus.

'Got a nice phone for you. Just get them to reconnect it, no problem.'

In the afternoon another tap.

'You got a green phone in there?' says a neighbour.

'Is this it?'

'Yeah, right. I'll take it back.'

So Cyrrhus gives her a lift to the telephone exchange.
'I won't be able to work till the phone's put in. It'll
take two weeks so I'll just pay half the rent till then.'

He says, 'You should have "friends" who'd give you
£100 any time you need it, and you should build up a
little reserve of them.'

No thanks. She just wants clients, not to socialize and
be available to people like that. It sounds like Gemma's
world.

She gathers every bit of washable material in the
room and takes it to the launderette. It is in a shopping
centre she used when she lived with a Tanzanian guy
about a mile away. It reminds her of the past. On the
way back she meets Phil. He and his friends in a band
say she can use their phone any time she likes, they
aren't going to pay the bill anyway. They are nice guys
but she never goes that way again because she doesn't
want to start up any social contacts. She cleans every
inch of the room with disinfectant.

Mr Kitten arrives. John and Sue gave him her
address, unfortunately. He says his friend has a room
in Notting Hill she could have for less rent than this.
(She only told Kitten half the rent she was paying.)

'But I like this room. I want this room and I'm going
to do massage here.'

'You're sure you're not doing anything wrong? You
see, I only want to help you.'

She sleeps alone on her own bed with the pure, clean
smells.

Next time she goes out she turns the other way,
down Peachy Hill, and discovers Peachy Hill village.
She stocks up on rubbers discreetly by buying little

packets at all three chemists'. Forcing herself to walk past the supermarket, she finds a health-food shop and buys herb teas and pure orange juice. She finds red grape juice. It's in a wine-coloured matt package with six languages on it.

Back home, the place has heated up beautifully. She takes her clothes off and drinks the red juice. A drop falls tastefully on her left breast and she looks at red and white together.

Too soon, Kitten comes round.

'You look different, sort of peaceful.'

'Yes, I am, I'm doing self-hypnosis.'

'Oh, you must be careful. Those sort of things are dangerous. You'll go funny in the head,' and he shakes his unkittenish head.

It doesn't feel right, his being in the room.

'No, I'm fine. You see, I've never lived by myself before and I just want to be completely alone so I can really enjoy it.'

He can't understand but at least she's told him and she doesn't think, this time, he'll ever come back.

She gets a big round mirror in Peachy Hill. She struggles back with it and props it up against the wall. As she looks in it, she doesn't like what she sees. But she doesn't mind her eyes being blue now; she used to hate her fair skin and blue eyes. But all the men she's known have had brown eyes, or black eyes, which somehow compensated.

'A woman like you should never be alone. I wanna help. I wanna help. I wanna help.' On her tiny radio someone's silly cries to help are weakened.

A black man arrives with a white phone. Her first telephone. She caresses it. Writes message cards to stick in newsagents'. A London Transport bus map shows likely places. She remembers a few places Harry Hello and Barnaby Budge used and decides on a couple of others. She's never put a card in by herself before, and feels dead scared.

In the first one there's a middle-aged woman looking compressed with a scowl instead of a smile. She buys *Horoscope* and splits. The next one is a politely smiling Pakistani. She hangs around the magazine rack. The other customer leaves. It's now or never. She goes up to the counter and whips one of the cards out of a little packet.

'How much for four weeks?'

'Forty pence. Thank you very much.'

'Thanks. Bye.'

Breakthrough.

Purple Prick's scare stories are still flickering in her mind. That day she places six cards. It's cheaper in the suburban newsagents, and they're less suspicious. Nearer town they look you up and down and charge ten times as much.

From a call box she phones Purple Prick and tells him he's a half-arsed cunt and other bits of information. He'll never be able to threaten her again. She enjoys the phone call and the queue outside the box does too.

Back home the telephone rings. She puts it in a cupboard and muffles it with cushions. She'll start tomorrow when she's ready. The phone purrs happily away. Some time in the afternoon she washes her face and showers, answering the telephone every now and then. She feels softly clean and contented. She gets a few appointments lined up. Some aren't going to happen and some are.

The buzzer goes, and opening the colourful door she feels a real smile warming up her face. Showing the client through the hall she notices its catty smell, but as she opens her door, the smell is of another world. She locks the door and takes the money. She watches him taking his clothes off.

'Is it all right to put them down there?'

'Yes, that's fine.'

He lies face down on the bed while she starts a token massage. At Barnaby's and Harry's she had the client on her right. Now she sits with the client on her left. His skin is quite nice, smooth with a bit of a tan, so she talks about where he's come from. Then she says he can turn over. She takes her top off and shakes her bra off and rubs him with her nipples, while she talks about them. Then, without much ado, he comes over his navel. From his sperm he looks like a heavy meat-eater, which reminds her that since around the time of Claude, she's been eating Kentucky Fried Chicken. She'll stop that and become purely vegetarian. Nothing but pure and beautiful food in this room. She gives him tissues and while she answers the phone and combs her hair he puts his rubbish away and dresses. They kiss goodbye and he'll be back now that he's found her. She can feel an even warmer smile on her face. She answers the phone again as she dresses. She washes and creams her hands.

The next guy darts in. He has nervous eyes and nose.

'Is it safe?' he says, his eyes darting into all corners of the room.

'Yes, of course.' She wonders what he means.

As he undresses, he relaxes and becomes more amiable. He wants to please her in every way possible. She's pleased and happy, anyway. He massages most parts of her and she feels refreshed and soothed. She contemplates the interesting scars on his body. He likes to take a long time and she starts to get bored and frustrated because the phone is ringing, and she's not able to reach it. She clothes him in a rubber and they move away from time. He smiles, she smiles, with a laugh.

'Check there's no one in the hall.'

'It's all clear.'

Then they kiss goodbye and he disappears. She takes a tissue and with it picks up the rubber garment containing his remains. She washes and creams her hands and combs her hair and feels a new self. Puts on jeans, feels like a walk.

On the way out she says Hello to another tenant. No response. She walks down Peachy Hill.

The buzzer sounds. She's not expecting any more appointments. She must be very careful to tell people they can only come if they phone and book.

He has pinkish skin and mousy hair and eyes. He says he's a virgin and he's eighteen; he doesn't want sex, he only wants to be wanked. She thinks it must be really strange to talk about sex if you've never had it. He's very nervous and it makes her nervous. When she's got rid of him she goes to a take-away shop and gets some containers of food. Too many for one person. She washes her face and showers. She puts her nylon sleeping bag on the bed, zips herself up in it and, with the radio on, eats all the food.

Meanwhile, the social worker who doesn't think she looks like a mother has arranged for her to have monthly access visits to her boys in Frillingford. She's very happy. Now there's no court case to think of. Nothing to distort this room. She'll just work here as much or as little as she wants.

A client pumps, squeezes and caresses her. She wonders at the combination of wrestling and dance.

A dream of Bill and Ben on her knee looking like babies but speaking like adults. Awake, she focuses on them as babies and toddlers and starts trying to imagine them at the ages they are now.

Coming out of the train at Frillingford she relaxes with self-hypnosis as she walks. Vera Lynn and Mrs Whitehouse merge in the smile of the stepmother who awaits her.

'Clover?'

'Yes.'

'They're in the park.'

In a sunlit park up the road the stepmother sits discreetly on a distant bench, and Clover meets Bill and Ben for the first time in five years.

'Hi.' And they kiss. She can feel the stepmother's worries hitting her from a distance as she sits on the bench, pretending everything is all right. Clover, Bill and Ben sit on the grass. She has been told they don't remember her. Ben says, 'I remember you tucking me in bed.'

'D'you remember the beach?' says Clover to Bill.

Bill's eyes say Yes and his mouth says No, as it's been told to.

They play with a football for a while and whirl round on a maypole, giggling. The stepmother serves them a big tea in her house, with her own children. Clover notices a purple bra among a pile of newly washed clothes. She tries to imagine the stepmother having sex, but can't.

Bill and Ben kiss her bye-bye and she'll phone tomorrow. Next time she'll see them they'll have moved to Blodminster.

A few dreams later, Bill and Ben have grown to their current ages.

Monday, her herbalized tongue blends with a client's peppermint-chewing-gum-over-nicotine one. While she massages him she learns there really is a pole at the North Pole – he's just been up it fixing something that the RAF, who were stationed there, should have been able to do anyway.

Next phone call is Eric. Shit! He's got the number from John and Sue, but he doesn't know the address. His friendly voice is a threat to her. She's scared, but she must tell him what she wants.

'Look, I'm not seeing anyone at all for a while. That's what I really want to do. I just want to be by myself. I've never been by myself before.'

'But I'm not anyone.'

'Yes, but I'm not seeing you or anyone.'

A reprieve, but he'll ring back.

She collects her things from the cupboard at John and Sue's.

'Good luck in your new place,' says the black taxi driver, helping her carry stuff into the hall, as if he's personally blessing her and the room.

Everything is unpacked for the first time since she was given suitcases by a charity in Sydney, when she was at the day-care centre. She unpacks it all now without hesitation. It's mostly clothes. Clothes people have given her because she didn't have any, clothes stolen or from dustbins, or swapped. Nine different kinds of foundation stolen or swapped, the fake fingernails of the dead wife of a guy she lived with once. None of the things that she really liked, that she would choose, were there. She's never chosen till now. They were just to keep her going; not for long, but a few weeks. She's never felt she'd last longer than that, has not felt strong enough. Now she feels the beginning of strength in her arms. Her hands pass through these foreign objects and feel a smooth stone – her beach stone. Her fist clenches round it. It has a beautiful grain. Someone said it might be fossilized wood. She gazes at it happily, puts it on a carved shelf in the corner. An African basket from a mission goes under the bed – to put the money in.

The phone rings. The guy doesn't say anything. She waits for him to hang up. It's the weekend, she'll put the phone in the cupboard. She's going to work Monday to Friday. She's never done that before. She wonders what her weekends will be like.

The buzzer sounds. It's Barnaby. Shock, horror. He's wanting to make sweet money with her again. He's got a real nice place to start work in.

'Are you with a guy here?' he says.

'Yes,' she says instinctively. It's the right answer.

He gives a number to contact, if she wants to work for him, then he's off pretty smartly. She gives him time to get away, then walks down Peachy Hill and gets a take-away from an Indian restaurant, and stretches out on her sleeping bag. As she does self-hypnosis Shell-water Beach still isn't there. She expects it'll turn up again some time.

Early Monday, and the first guy moves well, his skin is smooth and clean and she feels free and floating. Then she curls up with a James Baldwin book, answers the phone and eats some avocados.

The next one has a nice tan over firm muscles and when she releases him he explodes with a force which makes the room vibrate. When he's gone the room becomes hers again. She finishes the avocado, which she had put in the cupboard. Its greenness freshens up her mouth after his nicotine.

A call from Eric.

'How's your love life?'

'I'm not having one. I told you. I'm not seeing people apart from work.' She tries to explain to him again that she simply wants to be by herself. It's too simple for him to understand or believe, but at least he accepts that he can't understand. He also accepts that she has the right to do it, which she's very grateful for. But his phone call has intruded on the room and he may phone again and that bugs her.

Perhaps she should find another flat – one with a bath, her own entrance so she can open the door naked if necessary, a lower rent so it won't matter when she doesn't work, and the three people who know her phone number won't be able to bother her.

A letter forwarded from Gideon in Australia. Gideon had wanted to marry her. He was going to kill himself if she didn't. Nodi often threatened to kill her anyway. Lying on Shellweather her mind got nearer to thinking, so she stayed there with Gideon, because of that and because she couldn't have him suffer, and because she never wanted to go back to England where Nodi wanted to go. Shellweather was the first place she felt she belonged.

Gideon is in England, for five last days. At the tube station she smiles and they hug. She finds, as with Jed, that it doesn't feel as if he's been away. She takes him to Highgate Cemetery and they sit on grassy graves and eat blackberries. She thinks the blackberries might have been nurtured by the corpses under the greenery. She looks at Gideon and feels that he enjoys the thought too.

'I've never had sex with anyone since you. You're the only person I've ever had sex with.'

She doesn't know quite how to take that. It's a pity, really; he's a deeply sexy guy, with a virginal smell.

'I like this place, there's a good feeling here,' he says.

'Not like the rest of London.'

'You look really in bloom now.'

Once, when she'd left him, he described her as a moth flying towards the sun. Now he says she's "in bloom', whatever that means.

As they go into 3 Peachy Rise the room changes to become the room she's living in, not working in. She tells him she's not having sex with friends for a while. She's not having social contacts. He understands. They talk about the beach in Australia. He had heard that it had been virtually destroyed by a tidal wave. They chat on a while before it sinks in.

'Hey, Gideon! When did you say the tidal wave happened?'

'Er . . . it must have been May or June when my mum wrote me.'

So that's what happened to her beach. She tells him how she saw it disappear.

'They're trying to reclaim it.'

'Then I'll be able to see it again.' And they laugh.

Next day, they take a taxi to Heathrow and they'll see each other again but it doesn't matter why, where or when.

She gets the driver to take her to a vegetarian restaurant, where she has a summery meal. A friendly red bus straight up to Peachy Hill village. Gideon saw her through the bright-coloured glass. She hardly touches the tatty hall and goes into the soothing room.

* * *

'What colour pubic hair?' Wait, she wants time to adjust. She gulps at a glass of grape juice and then returns to the phone.

'Yes, an appointment lasts up to half an hour.'

She opens a packet of almonds.

'But I always take exactly half an hour to come.'

She chews some almonds.

'Then you can make a double appointment.'

She examines some other almonds. Little engraved works of art.

The first one has taken an afternoon off to enjoy himself. They kiss and, as their clothed bodies embrace, he hands her the money subtly so as not to break the embrace. She moves him towards the cupboard to place it under her peppermint tea box. She likes the room. He soothingly massages her breasts, unbuttons her top, moves her bra so her nipples are exposed. She likes her nipples too. She doesn't need a place with a bath and a separate entrance. The shower is fine.

'You look so sweet.'

He's trying to reach her cunt through her clothes. She takes some layers off to prevent them being messed up. As she rubs herself against his hardened trousers, she thinks, Jed hasn't got my phone number, with luck, and will forget my address with his next NHS fix. She throws her bra at the mirror and feels her comforting skin.

'You're beautiful. You're fantastic. What a body.' He licks what he thinks is her clitoris. If Eric rings it won't affect her. She has told him she's being alone. She's never had the chance before. The client kisses her tummy. Gideon will be at the other end of the world for a long, long time. She stretches, turns over, searching for a rubber in the box under the bed. Turning round,

she squeezes, licks, strokes and sucks the delicate pink
rubber over his welcomely clean cock. John and Sue are
unlikely to phone her. Even if they do they will be easy
to put off. He licks and kisses her face. Behind her
closed eyes and moistened face she thinks that no one
else knows where she is. He moves his hips with a
good rhythm and she joins him, building up the
rhythm. She knows she is here where she wants to be.
This is it. She doesn't have to move again. The truth
dawns on her, her whole body. This is what and where
she wants to be.

'You enjoyed that, didn't you?'

'Mm? Oh, yeah.' She smiles, but what she is enjoying is beyond him. Putting on pants, bra, cotton skirt,
and T-shirt, she watches him pee and wash. She combs
her hair as he puts on the clothes which say what
he 'is'. When she has shut the door after him, she
washes her hands in privacy and puts almond cream
on them.

She polishes the mirror with Windolene. Then she
sits and focuses on her face, making it stronger and
calmer. It begins to glow. She looks at it and 'she'
becomes 'I'. Her face becomes 'me'. I'll stay here and
work when I choose. I'll have no social contacts or do
anything that could lead to social contacts. I'll see my
kids every six weeks or so, but that's OK. They're
moving to a town I've never been to. Neither they nor
their father and stepmother know anyone where I'm
known. They don't know where I am. No one, no past
or would-be friends know where I am, except clients
and they won't know who I am. It's beautiful.

I'll stay here . . . till I want to have contact with
people . . . till I am what I want to be . . . till I can be

myself. My eyes start to penetrate my face in the mirror, then they take in the room. Pink and white tissues containing a used rubber lie on the floor. I put them in the blue and white pedal bin and wash my hands.

6

'You Must Be Lonely'

'You sound very young.'

'I'm twenty-three.' I choose an age that they'll believe.

'Where do you come from?'

'England.' Or wherever, depending on what mood I'm in. Maybe they mean am I white or coloured, but don't like to say so.

'What size bust?' I choose a number.

When I'm working I attach myself to the vibrating telephone. Although I make appointments each day and for that day only, I never really know if – or when – they'll turn up. When I finish in the evening, I tuck up the telephone in the cupboard with cushions to quieten it. Or, if I want to finish working at any time, I do that. If I feel like going out, I go out, and sometimes the telephone is tucked up for days on end while I travel around London looking at normal life. My appointment times connect me to chronological time, but whenever I want, I step out of it and move like liquid in liquid.

A client comes over my face for extra money. It is his 'fantasy'. The first bit is warm, then it turns quite cool. I think it should be the other way round. I think of an ancient British custom of putting a mare's placenta on a bush, and feel briefly like a bush.

After I close the door I wash my face, put wheat-germ lotion on it, scoop up and check and smell the peppermint-scented notes from under the box. I take out the telephone and stretch out on the bed. A cup of peppermint tea sends steam towards me and I wriggle my feet in the mirror.

Prr. Prr.

Silence. No wanking, no heavy breathing, nothing. I keep motionless and silent, and after a long time out-silence it and hear a receiver click.

'Are you big?'

'Are you small?'

'Is that the Nat West Bank?'

'Do you come?'

'Do you enjoy it?'

'Is your cunt made of diamonds?'

I let in a long, thin, greyish client with a middle-class London smell. He hasn't eaten or smoked recently so kissing him doesn't get through my peppermint aura. He takes off his lower clothes and I take off my upper ones. His shirt and tie have to be protected by a rainbow of coloured tissues as he sprays over his navel. He invites me to accompany him on business trips.

'No, I don't go on holidays. If I move, I never go back.'

My next move will be far, far away. How could I be with him for more than the structured half hour?

Next appearance is a heavy, bulging alcoholic who wants to do more for less. I gently open the door again for him. He stands there bulging heavily and aggressively and threatens me with the police as his porky pink cock appears. I open the door wider and he gets his semi-exposure and more police threats through it. I hope his threats will disappear as his erection does. I'm not ready to leave this place yet, I think, as I flick through a James Baldwin book, and my stomach, filled with only peppermint tea, synchronizes with hunger in New York.

Next one's steamy with nicotine and his prick smells, looks and must taste like an ashtray. I flick him over, as lightly as possible. It's easy because he's relaxed, and happy about sex. He's just had a peppermint chewing gum so, when we kiss, synthetic and organic flavours combine. As he's dressing and I'm brushing my hair, he spots the James Baldwin book.

'Oh! You read him too, do you?'

'Yes.'

'Yeah, he's a good author, I think. But what gets me is, now that he's successful, he still harps on the blacker side of life – like he's bitter or something.'

I never put my library books on public display again.

At this time male gold jewellery is in fashion – wristwatches and lots of neckwear. Sagittarius, Aries, Leo, tigers' teeth, sharks' teeth, Capricorn, Taurus, Virgo, stars of David, Aquarius, Gemini, Libra, crucifixes, Pisces, Cancer, Scorpio, St Christophers, A – Zs, Virgin Marys and other metal symbols shake around throbbing neck veins. Sometimes I remember the symbol and sometimes a face.

Monday lunchtime and the buzzer gets me out of bed. A client I booked last week. I hide traces of my having been in bed here and let him in. I am massaged, kissed, caressed. I turn over. He powders and pampers my back. I am waking up and I flick the radio on – it's full of traffic conditions. He's smooth, gentle and polite. Nearly all of them are. I feel well treated. I wash and drink a new red tea. I relax more and more as I accommodate myself to unexpected shapes and movements. As I watch them peeing, washing and putting on their clothes I sometimes catch glimpses of who they 'are' in their world. People I would never associate with sex, or with me.

I find the most beautiful building-society building in London, swish through its sexy smoked-glass door and lay peppermint-scented notes on the counter.

On the bus I look at the clothes hiding the bodies and the way they move. I'm glad I work naked so that I can enjoy wearing clothes when I do wear them. If I wear clothes too much I feel less real. A black boy of about five is kicking an enormous cardboard box towards the bus and three guys are cheering and encouraging him. As they get up to leave, I see one of them is wearing striped, neatly fitting trousers in good colours and materials. He's reasonable-looking and well shaped and not old, but I know he looks better and more himself in his clothes than without them. I wonder about it.

Back home and my breasts are round, smooth rubber, my head is on a firm stomach and my thoughts drift around like little puffs of cloud.

The next client keeps staring into my eyes with hard curiosity. I remain relaxed and try to float myself away because his stare gets tedious after a while. He says, 'It's weird, it's freaky. How can you do this for a living?'

''Cos it's my job.'

'But why don't you do a normal job? This is weird, it must be bad for you.'

'Oh.'

The next one has a bulging, porous nose full of devious questions which could lead on to more questions. He doesn't get any answers.

'You don't have the usual line of patter, do you?'

'Don't I?'

'Are you tall?'

'Can I bring my thirteen-year-old brother?'

'I'm coloured. D'you mind?'

I tuck the phone up and am now in my private room.

I have a dream in which I see the lower half of a guy wearing tight striped trousers which actually blend into and become his arse so he has an arse made of pinstripe material. He is being fucked by a disembodied prick in matching pinstripe material. In the morning I see the dream as the logical conclusion of people becoming the clothes they wear.

The telephone wakes up and soon I put it next to me till I'm ready to answer it.

Prr. Prr.

I sense it's not the usual call. It's the mate of the racing driver whom I was going to share a flat with. He's heard I do massage and tracked my number, he needs one because his back is playing up. I arrange to see him at his place. It's strange being in someone else's room. I act very straight and give him a straight massage for a straight massage price. As his erection mounts I realize I can't do anything to him because it's not the right place and I've met him before. I act very polite and drink tea which has a corrupt taste. He wants a few more massages, so I tell him I'm moving and I'll call him from my new number. That should protect me from any future contact with him.

I do self-hypnosis on a train across London and my hurtling body becomes soft and floating. When I come to, my eyes feel stronger and I look through the window at sharper colours. A little man sits opposite with a big erection creeping along one thigh. I continue my thoughts through the window. He keeps popping his head from behind his newspaper. A few stops later it dawns on me, I'm expected to look at his erection. It has nothing to do with me so I go on facing it but not seeing it. When he has to get out, he shoots one more glance as he walks down the platform, but I still look unseeing.

At Peachy Hill village I buy mangoes, avocados, magazines and fruit juices.

Back home I stretch out my legs, am licked for a long time. I stretch my arms above my head.

'Why are you laughing?'

'I'm just smiling, that's all.'

'How many clients do you have a day then?'

'Oh, it depends.'

'Well, on average?'

'Not too many. I like to keep things quiet, you know.'

'What do you do between appointments? You must get lonely here when you're by yourself.'

'Oh, it's all right,' I reassure him. 'I answer the phone a lot, read magazines, write letters, usually I have a telly to watch, and I ring my friends.'

I don't tell him the truth – that most of the time I just am, and for the first time don't need to do anything. I let him out. I see another tenant walking through the hall. How long will it be before they find out? I put the client's remains in the plastic refuse bag and tie it all tightly, remembering Purple Prick's stories. I put the bag in the dustbin in the back garden. Nothing can be seen through the plastic except fruit juice containers. I swish and crunch some leaves. I say Hello to another tenant, but get no reply. This is good. Perhaps I can keep my privacy here.

Inside I take my clothes off. I can hear noises of other people in the house and outside. I look at myself in the mirror. If I'm quiet, they'll never get to me, I hope. I shower and squash half a mango over my face and eat the other half. I flick through *Time Out*, through the things people do to 'enjoy' themselves. I look at the colours and light of my room, enjoy it as much as I want to and lick mango off myself. Someone is going on about loneliness on the radio. How is it possible to be lonely? I wonder. I'm the opposite – but there's no word for it.

I stroke the bedspread. It's pretty and makes me happy. There is so much here. If I were blind I might feel lonely. The people I've known could last me, if I never saw anyone for the rest of my life. I'm full up with people but I couldn't give up my eyesight.

Next day I walk, clean-jeaned, down Peachy Hill and get a bus. If I shop at different shops, people won't recognize me too much, and I wear different clothes when I'm working.

It must be Saturday, because people are shopping in couples. They are still affected by Friday night and have to prepare themselves for Saturday night. I'm glad I've escaped from all the couples I've been in, but a bit guilty that I'm luckier than they are. I've never had to believe in Saturday, or any other day.

I eat at a vegetarian restaurant and look at clothes. Different shops have different music. With my radio I can have music at work only when I want and don't have to live with other people's noises.

I get back, wash body, face and hair and tuck into my newly laundered sleeping bag and personal nylon sheets. My working quilt is waiting for next week. People upstairs are quarrelling and eating food, steam comes down the stairs. I feel beautiful. No one is coming to see me. No more forced awakenings by people I might not want to be with. No one can possess my thoughts.

Monday again, and I walk down Peachy Rise to buy litres and litres of fruit juice. I live on fruit juice for a few days and my insides feel sweet enough to over-power some of the clients' smells, and outside, through the traffic fumes, I can smell fruit and vegetables in shops.

That weekend I go to Blodminster to see my kids. I get bruises all over my calves from fourteen dodgem-car rides. We bash as many others as possible. In the evening, staying at a bed-and-breakfast place, I watch telly with the landlord and landlady. They think I'm a receptionist. What would they do if I suddenly started wanking him?

7

'Are You Frightened?'

A weight lowers itself on to my chest, I let my limbs go rag-doll limp and I learn to breathe without moving my ribcage. My mind and body float.

This act could be so many things. If I were in South America being held forcibly for days in temperatures too high, or too low, and had various things done to me, it would be rape and torture.

If it happened here in England in tolerable surroundings with this guy, only at times chosen by him, and if it was all I had for pleasure, it would be tough luck.

In my situation, it's a living.

A client with red hair and grey roots and a bullet wound a hair's breadth from his balls. He goes on and on about how beautiful I am. His near miss is interesting. I love scars. He got it in some war. I lick it for a while and think about Prince and the photo of him in his cell in America. I have a letter unopened from him in the cupboard. The client talks about movies he's connected with.

Prr. Prr.

'Er. Excuse me, but is that a massage parlour?'

'Um. Yes. I thought so. We're having a lot of joke calls today. I'm a locksmith, you see, and we've had a half-dozen hoax calls so far today, all to massage parlours.'

We talk about massaging and locksmithing and he comes round for an appointment. He has a double appointment and in between cuddling we spend most of the time talking about his schooldays. What a strange way to spend one's money.

I put his spermy tissues in the bin, wash my hands, comb my hair and smell my money.

I walk down Peachy Rise and Peachy Hill. I'm in my outside clothes now. My skin feels fresher and I'm aware of the touch of materials around my body. I skirt cold Saturday sick on the Monday pavement.

A mother is walking down the street. She is dragged down and hung on to by two children, a pushchair and things she has had to buy. Maybe she will never be free. On the bus I look at the sky. The conductor is dragged down by his uniform and metal clipping machine. His body is spoiled and jolted by the bus.

Back home I open Prince's letter. Rather than battle uselessly to get his case retried, he thinks he might get a TV set to watch till they let him out. He says something about seeing me when he's out. It's ironic – although I want him to get out I don't want him or anyone else to see me in the foreseeable future. So if he weren't in prison we wouldn't write.

Next day I send him money for a telly. I buy one for myself. I've never had such a massive object before. A greyish rectangular man appears on it. I twiddle brightness and contrast and his contour lines, bones, hairs, moles and pores appear and disappear until I get a satisfactory texture.

I sit on the bed and look at the eyes, mouth. He's one of the greyish, more or less rectangular men, probably suffering from too much contact with his greyish, more or less rectangular car. Before I was working I never thought of them as human, I was hardly aware of them. Now I can look at his face and see bits of humanity and curves. He's reading the news.

I remember a book about the Tristan da Cunhans who were erupted from their island, the remotest in the world, by a volcano and had to stay in England till it was safe to go back. One of them was amazed that we needed news so often, because they only had it twice a year by boat.

I look through *Private Eye*, and send off for a catalogue of rubbers. They come in all shapes, sizes and colours. I think it would be a good investment to buy them wholesale now.

I twiddle with the telly again and get marvellous textures of skin. I shower, climb into my soft, nylon, blue cocoon which changes the room from a working place to a private place, switch off the light and sink into the new, delicious joy of being by myself, safe, free and unknown. I've turned the sound low enough so that even my telly-watching will be unknown to others in the house. Perhaps I can start to get into telly. This must be what people mean by 'settling down'.

I buy my first iron. It's a travelling one.

I take a bus to Regent's Park. I'm glad the bus is red as there's a lot of greyness around. I walk through Regent's Park. Last time I was here, it seemed a cruel place, artificial. I'd just been thrown out of an au pair job after three weeks and had been picked up and had my wages – all I had in the world – ripped off. I was standing still wondering where to go – should I go back to King Wanker? He was a guy who believed in pure wanking with an almost religious fervour. He used drugs to prevent erections and orgasms and got Vaseline everywhere.

This time I see it's full of deciduous trees laying their leaves messily around. Deciduous trees seem like clients

who try to prolong it as much as possible and so keep
going up and down. I like gum trees and palm trees.

In the middle of Baker Street, a black guy is freaking
out in anger. He's in the middle of the one-way system.
I want to go over to him but I think he'd get angrier, so
I go into a shop by the vegetarian restaurant. Everyone
is acting like good little children whose naughty brother
is being told off.

As I walk up Peachy Hill again, a car slows down
beside me. I hope it's not a client who recognizes me.
They shouldn't in my outside clothes. I put on a
disappearing look and go home.

I take some tissues and muffle the phone bell with
them. Now the ring is a soft purr and can be silenced
completely with a cushion.

One guy wants his nipples pinched really hard. I
can't do that, it gives me too much pain. Afterwards I
think, If I've felt other people's pain all my life, I should
be able to feel their pleasure. Next time he comes I
pinch his nipples with my strongest nails and it's
bearable.

'Do you come?' a client says.

'Oh yes, sometimes.' Which sounds suitable.

Then he caresses, licks and massages me gently. 'Is
this all right?'

'Hard enough, soft enough?'

'Do you like this?'

He needs me to 'enjoy' myself and I do enjoy myself.

I loll pantless, with a white skirt flouncing around my
legs, watching a client.

'You don't mind, I've brought my own – if that's
OK?'

'Yeah, that's fine.'

He adorns himself with rubbers, one after the other –

first a white one, then a black one, then a rainbow-coloured one (the first one I've seen, very pretty – my catalogue from the *Private Eye* ad has got these in) and last of all one like a hot-water bottle with bits on. I remember my friend Jackanory going on a shoplifting spree through London's sex shops and bringing back bits and pieces in plastic and rubber which I pretended to enjoy since he'd gone to such trouble to get them.

This time I don't pretend. I enjoy being amused. He comes, I put on my pants again, pull them up tightly against me, take them off again as he wants to buy them.

I reattach myself to the phone as I choose the next pair of pants to wear. I have a crimson silk pair halfway up my legs, while someone wants to know my measurements.

'91-61-91.'

'Eh? You must be joking!'

'We're supposed to be decimalized, you know.' But they're not yet programmed to be aroused by centimetres.

I angle myself towards the mirror to see what my face looks like, answering the phone, and I lift the other leg through the silk crimson. I flick through *Spare Rib*, *Private Eye*, *Time Out* and clients.

The buzzer sounds and I smile out at a black African with a briefcase. I try to look as if I know him already because a fellow tenant is hanging around the hall. The client, being African, is spotlessly clean. I have decided to get a take-away vegetable biriani, come back, reclaim my room, wash, shower, jump in my cocoon and eat the take-away in time to watch *The Sweeney*. The client bites my nipple and I'm taken back to before Peachy Rise and being bitten in freezing rooms in north and east London – sometimes with broken teeth. I thank whoever is responsible that I am now a prostitute. I tell the client that I don't like being bitten. While he massages me instead, I think about my black-social white-commercial sex syndrome being broken. Now everyone who comes here is work. It gives the room a purity of function.

I run to the take-away with the virtuous feeling of having done a full day's work. I wonder if any of the guys working there are clients, or are they just looking at me? It's interesting. I whip back to reclaim my room.

It's grey and gently rainy today. There are lots and lots of phone calls but no action. Voices appear and disappear. I'm not very sensitive to voices so I try to become aware of the different accents and intonations. Sometimes one sounds like someone I've known. Perhaps it is. One sounds like Cyrrhus, the landlord. Perhaps it's him checking up on me.

'I'm a virgin, do you mind?'

'I'm eighty-two, do you mind?'

'I've a problem – a fifteen-inch prick. Do you mind?'

I sound as if I believe them.

I've noted down a few appointments for later on: they're not very certain ones. I go through the rain to buy some food. In the almost overwhelming greyness, people's skin colours are sharply revealed. I notice men in phone boxes and buy some cheesecake, so tender it can hardly stand up, and a beginner's guide to radio. In the Indian shop I see some fat pink incense.

'It helps you meditate and get in touch with God,' the guy says.

At home I dry my feet, which have turned a nice ivory. I light four sticks of incense and lick cheesecake.

'Sound is caused by vibrations,' the book says. I listen

to vibrations coming through my receiver, through the intense drizzle, from all over London.

Buzzer goes. Hide cheesecake, hide book, lick cheesecake off lips, jump into silver shoes and white flouncy skirt. It's a very regular client. He has barely got his trousers off when he aims his erection at my left foot. I sink gracefully into a sitting position on my bed. He rubs his cock over my shoe and foot. Which is it, foot or shoe? I wonder. He takes the shoe and licks it hysterically and rolls around the floor wanking himself. I'm dying to finish the cheesecake.

'Quick, quick, get a rubber. I'm going to come.'

I just manage to catch his orgasm with a rubber and he heaves in a final massive clinch with my shoe. Then he subsides, takes a tissue, wipes himself and neatly puts it in the bin.

'Yes, I don't know why it comes over me like that. It seems to coincide with a full moon, on the whole.'

I watch him combing his thin, grey hair with my largest Afro comb. He picks up his briefcase, attaches himself to his car keys, and I see him out and get back to the cheesecake. The incense is creating a deep, full-bodied, rose-coloured atmosphere.

Buzzer again. Back into the cupboard with the cheesecake. Phone rings. It's someone saying nothing so I leave it off the hook and go barefoot to the door. A thin, rigid guy darts in.

'Can you close the curtains, please?'

'OK.'

I put the light on.

'Do you work?' he says.

'Yes, this is my job.'

'No, I mean at anything apart from this.'

'No.'

'You're not a student?'

'No.'

'You look like a student. You sure you're not a student?'

'Why do you think I am?'

'It's that biro,' he says, eyeing a silver-plated one I found in Claude Catsilk's drawer. 'Why do you have an expensive biro? You see, I notice things. I look at people.'

'I like looking at people.'

'You like to suss people out?'

'I like looking at people.'

'You see, I'm in a position of great authority over people and I need someone to go to regularly to exert authority over me. I want domination, real domination, verbal domination.'

He lies down on the carpet and I walk aimlessly over him and slap him a few times in a half-hearted way, but I don't give him 'verbal domination', because I don't like to have to talk to someone unless I want to, and I don't want him to come back. He comes feebly into his hand.

Finally I finish the cheesecake and drink red grape juice and eat a tin of giant marrowfat processed peas.

Soon my legs are entwined around the neck of a guy who's kneading my stomach. I look happily at my legs. I identify most with them. The place is thick with rose incense by now and all the room feels soft and pink.

'Aren't you frightened?'

'Of what?'

'Well, anyone could come round, couldn't they? You don't know what they're going to do, do you? You must get some funny ones. You must get frightened. Mustn't you?'

'It's better than crossing the road.'

When I've closed the door behind him I turn the light off and sit on the bed contemplating the telly and four stubs of glowing incense. I've earned my privacy again. A period starts, to coincide with the weather. I tuck myself up happily with blood and rain pouring.

As I put the first notes of the next day into the African basket, I remember the guy last night saying, 'Aren't you frightened?' Each time I earn money, I think it's a gamble, they could bop me on the head and pinch the whole lot. This heightens the value of the money for me, and gives more luck to my job. As I lead the next client in and he doesn't bop me on the head, I have all the pleasure of winning a gamble.

On the bed, one is stretching all his limbs across me in an exaggerated way, and asking how he pleases me. It excites me to think that he could reach one arm under the bed and run off with the week's takings.

I quieten the phone and look through magazines. There's a photograph of women in a refuge for battered wives. I recognize the expecting-to-be-hit look in a woman's face as the camera clicked suddenly. I've dropped that feeling now. Nodi was frightening when he was drunk, but since I was in fear and cold anyway it didn't feel personal. The last time I felt a tinge of fear as someone came through a door was at Claude Catsilk's but at that time I didn't know I was still frightened. Now I know what a condition of fear I lived in.

I fill my old suitcases with most of my borrowed, given, stolen, swapped and found clothes, an electric fire, a copy of *Jaws*, a bottle of whisky – the last two given to me by clients. How can I get them out of here? I take a minicab. There's the germ of a new feeling of being able to do things, to make things happen. Sitting next to the driver in the minicab, I notice that I chat to him easily. It's the feeling of being able to pay someone for something, too.

We go up the steps to a door with new locks on it. It's opened cautiously. Two women look nervously at the driver and less nervously at me. Then I'm inside the door, having paid the guy. There aren't enough clothes to go round. I wonder what else I can bring them. A little boy gets *Jaws* and we talk about the film, which I saw with my kids. A woman is shuddering and crying and telling her story to someone and kids are playing in the garden.

Outside there are bomb scares. Inside, I dance across clients.

'What colour knickers you got on?'

'Pardon?'

'What colour knickers you got on?'

'Pink.'

It was fascinating. The caller's words and inflections were always the same, however much I tried to vary the response – even if I said I'd been chatting with his mother the other day. He might have been a questioning machine.

I'm using up black rubbers while I wait for my wholesale order. As I'm sucking a guy off I wonder how he'll react when he sees it doesn't match. I stand up and he looks down at his fallen cock.

'D'you get these from the council then? It looks like a council rubbish bag.'

We giggle.

'I'm a fireman,' says one.

'Oh.'

He comes steaming in, then subsides and kind of snorts a bit.

'Yeah, well, look – do you mind if I go? You see – er – I only came because I had a row with the wife. See, I jus' came here 'cos I was angry and, well, I don't think that's a good reason, really.'

'No, I agree with you. That's OK.'

At the door he says, 'Look, you could just give me a massage, nothing more, for half the price.'

'No, sorry.'

'One day you may need a fireman and then we won't come.' I have visions of being blacked by every fire brigade in London.

As I shut the door the phone rings. The cushion has fallen off it.

'Hello. This is Peachy Hill police.'

This is it, I think. My hands are sweating.

'We've had a complaint that you've been seen soliciting in Peachy Hill Park and we'd like to send two men over there to question you. Are you agreeable to that?'

'Uh.'

I wipe my left hand. It starts to sweat again. The receiver in my right hand is damp. I relax and try to think straight. Peachy Hill Park is at least a mile away from Peachy Hill village. I've only been there once, about three years ago, playing with some kids.

'Look, there must be some mistake. Yes, this is the right number but I've never been near Peachy Hill Park.' He agrees with me very easily.

'Oh, well, perhaps some punter came along and didn't rise to his own expectations. Huh huh huh!'

'Huh huh huh,' I agree with him. 'That could be it.'

He asks where I advertise and I tell him. He asks my name and address.

'Clover Star.' My old name. I don't say Dawn.

'Well, that's fine. We've no objection to you

advertising in shop windows. Only one thing, if you
move, let us know, won't you? We just like to keep an
eye on things. It's the best way, you know.'

'Yes, OK.'

I ask his name and rank and he tells me. Then we say
goodbye. I wipe both my hands. I remember when they
were sticky nearly all the time. I think through the
conversation. It's cool. It's OK. I'm secure to a certain
extent. If it was the police! Of course, it could have been
anyone. I'm more than 90 per cent sure that it was the
police. If it wasn't, someone I don't know has got my
private name connected with this address. But that
person wouldn't know I live here, only that I work
here. It's still OK. I'm almost sure he was genuine as I
go over it once more. I look at my dry hands. The nails
look good: the ridges and white spots have nearly gone.

At Blodminster I sit fully clothed with the landlady and
her husband. This is the only time I'm with people in a
domestic situation. In a way it slightly corrupts what
I'm doing to be in such an environment. They are
watching *Sale of the Century* and I enjoy it because they
do.

With Bill and Ben, I go to *The Towering Inferno*. It's
very sexy. People are trapped and tense in an enormous, burning tower block. Ten million tons of water
being released on the fire is one of the most beautiful
things I've seen. We see it again. Afterwards I just want
to see films about fire and water, with people in minor
roles.

8

'It Must Be Degrading'

Days of peace, days of silence. I don't have to speak unless I want to. Quiet days when I swirl around the bed making cosy little animal noises, and I watch them talking about the weather and the traffic and bits of me. I shut the door, brush them out of my hair, lie down on the floor (forgetting who has trodden there) and do self-hypnosis. The beach appears again – bleached and bedraggled but it's there.

The nights come sooner, the cold tap gets colder. I buy a lamp with cherubs on it. I have two large objects now, a lamp and a television. I buy mauve lace curtains to put over the white ones on the inside. The people in the shop are anxious whether I can afford them or not. I sit on the bed and watch the patterns of the mauve and white curtains merging. My life is focused on this bed now. I eat, sleep, work and relax on it. Three curtains and three doors protect me.

When I'm dressed I wear my own clothes, a flouncy pink skirt and white top. I look in the mirror and brush my hair, staring at my face. As I look, it grows stronger. I enjoy the intricacy of the curtains and the simplicity of the bed behind me.

A freckled back on the bed which I stroke gently. It looks quite helpless and I feel sorry for it. When I was little I had a fantasy about destroying everyone who was ugly. Fair and freckled people were, so they had to go. The back turns over and I smell the rank, fair armpit and the stale mouth. No point in trying to avoid a drop of sweat falling from the armpit. Afterwards I still smell clean and my mouth tastes the same. I'm surprised.

My feet stroke the rough carpet and I brush my hair. A black-haired client with beautifully shining eyes is padding his feet with socks and tying up sexy-textured shoes with spotless laces.

'Do you live here then?'

'No, I live in Putney.'

'That's all right then. It wouldn't be very good living here, would it?'

I cherish the room. On display only a bed, a mirror on the wall and two soft sofas. The surfaces are covered by fabrics, ornaments from fairgrounds, my beach stone and some magazines. The cupboards conceal new clothes, library books, my phone, bills, receipts, letters from Prince in prison, Co-op stamps, papers, letters and old photos.

A knock on the door. It's not a client. I wonder if it's Cyrrhus the landlord.

'You always seem so calm,' he says. He talks about putting the rent up and I watch him as he talks. He listens to me. We agree. His twin brother Pyrrhus is going to collect the rent from now on. He's like Cyrrhus but he has a birthmark on his face and is an accountant. Cyrrhus is concocting a story for Pyrrhus to explain my presence in the room, because Cyrrhus is working again and is going on a magical mystery tour. By the time he comes back I may be anywhere. I kiss him on the cheek.

'That was unexpected,' he says.

On a Saturday I take a bus to the building society. I wear clothes for outside – blue jeans, blue top.

A guy starts talking to me, trying to pick me up. I look at his cigarette, which is part of him. He acts as if he has something to offer me. He thinks I'm a student so I let him think that. When he asks my name I say nothing.

I'm not Dawn outside. I used to be Clover, but not now. I don't want a name just yet. He's nervous with his cigarette. Outside I don't want to be accompanied by anyone. I elude him.

The building society is just about to close. How soon will it be before all the black-uniformed men recognize me? Standing in the queue I watch the women and girls who work here. Week after week, they are there, trapped in angles and ugliness. Yet some are beautiful. How can they remain so? The digits of my account number add up to nine, my favourite number. Some of my banknotes have honey on them.

In the queue at the vegetarian restaurant I practise anonymity. The people working behind the counter look bored. How can they stay? Again, I feel guilty about my luck, the burdens I've escaped. Eating food away from my bed I notice the colours and textures of it on the plate and on the table.

Some Saturdays I go to Kensington Market. Then I escape to cleanliness and a Sunday fast. Some Sundays I lie in my blue sleeping bag remembering voices from the past. I start to understand the words, let them hurt me and then cry them away. I start to move my life around. I look forward to Monday.

A client with clean dirt on his hands. He happily releases his money, himself, his liquid. I get on with a letter to Prince. As I try to write, I imagine the prison officers devouring my words and photo.

'So slow, so gentle.' My skirt swirls around a client. He softens. I am soothed. He melts and subsides. Firmly I close the door and get the room to myself. He has left his newspaper, and it looks like an alien in this room. I don't get newspapers now. Little bits of news waft in from the radio or telly. That's enough. I don't like writing to Prince but I want to send him money sometimes. I finish the letter and take the cushion off the phone.

'How tall?'

'What size?'

I improvise and look at the newspaper lying on the bed. When I was at Claude Catsilk's, it was 'wrong' to put newspapers on the bed and 'right' to be in the bathroom having a shit if he was in the bath. A place before, a guy before, it was the other way round. And, before that, another set of rules and, before that, another and so on.

A meaty, bulky, blond guy is admiring his cock in my mirror. Under the glow of the cherub lamp he prances in worship. To Capital Radio he shadow-boxes with his cock, silhouetted on the wall. I imagine him in a room papered with his blown-up cock, in his element. I smile.

'Where do you come from?'

I laugh inside and wonder why he needs to know; I wouldn't if I were just about to fuck someone. I smell wet armpits. They ask, 'I'm not hurting you, am I? I don't want to hurt you. Don't let me hurt you.'

And, on a phone-in, people are joining in and helping each other all over London. Sudden unexpected gifts to children, housebound and handicapped people.

'If you charge me less, I'll come regularly/more often.'

'No.'

I don't want that. To be dependent on the money and the approval of a particular person.

Outside I post the letter. I taste the dark air and walk among clothed people. It's too dark to see the bodies beneath the clothes and I wonder why, with the money these people have, they don't buy more beautiful clothes. Back home I am touched by silence and enjoy the evening which I've earned.

Next day, I write out some more cards, rainbow-coloured, and take a bus to check the cards I've put up. Now I'm posing as 'one of them'. Some time in the future I ought to be with people, but, in a way, I'm fulfilling that obligation by being with clients. I look at my hands on my lap and lean my head against the window and feel the vibrations of the bus. I get up to get off the bus and clothed bodies move out of my way without my having to ask.

'Cheer up, then! It may never happen.'

At the newsagent's I check my card is still there. An old woman is serving behind the counter. I keep the card in my pocket.

'I want to renew a card, third up, fourth right.'

I wonder if she knows what it's about. The Indian owner is smiling in the background. Does he know me or recognize me? I get out on the street, but the owner is following me, I think. I get on a bus going to Hampstead and relax. I get off the bus and walk up the hill with unreal shops and unreal trees. A man with a red-veined face and sandy hair, which would be beautiful if it were clean, is surrounded by stinking bottles. He wants some money to buy food. So we go into one of the shops.

'I've told you you're not to come in here,' says the Indian owner.

'He's with me,' I say. I imagine what he'd look like if I could clean, soothe, dress, create him. I try to guess what he'd like. I get pork pies, brown bread, some butter, tomatoes, cheddar cheese and a fruit pie. I buy garlic cream cheese for myself.

'Bye-bye.'

I walk up Haverstock Hill eating the cheese. The denim of the blue jeans in the windows doesn't look real, either.

At home, black and red nylon lace which I'd saved from my life before, when it seemed too pretty to wear. I watch myself being fucked from behind in the clouded mirror. I think of a mare nonchalantly swishing her tail. Without the client knowing, I try to separate myself from the picture. I watch myself being fucked by rubbers, by smooth rubbers. Will he lose the rubber, miss me? I improvise. Am I different enough from him? I enjoy my new perfume.

Then I anoint the mirror with perfumed pink cream. He has left a king-size Virginia tip stub which lingers in the room. I empty it into the bin and, with rubber gloves, try to wash the tar off the gilt plate I use as an ashtray. Smell of tarred water. I wash my gloved hands.

'Shocking, isn't it?' they say about the weather.

A client takes off discreet grey trousers to reveal surprisingly fit legs. I sit on the legs and with my tongue and fingers enclose his cock in transparent rainbowed rubber. In rhythm to Capital, in tune with London, yeh, yeh, yeh, I tongue the masked organ and look at the mantelpiece through the sexagon made by our thighs.

I go down Peachy Rise crushing fading brown leaves. I buy avocados, nuts. People talk about prices but I've never known much about them. I can buy things now, but I need less than when I couldn't have anything. I look and enjoy the pretty coloured packets of cigarettes, the ones I couldn't afford to think about then. Now I enjoy the colours and names and don't need them.

'Cheer up, love.'

In the Oxfam shop I skim through the fusty clothes and look at the old women on guard. I'd like to change and soften their faces. In the unaccustomed mirror I look different. I try on a long pink coat and we merge in the mirror. I watch them disapproving and I pay what they ask.

It smells clean but I'll dry-clean it. Now I have something I really like to wear. I remember uncomfortable unliked clothes that I had no choice about. Both the clothes and people hurting. This coat feels made for me. I get *Paradise Papers* from the library.

Back home I take off and put away the blue jeans. I swirl about in the room.

Soft, brown eyes and clean, soft, spicy skin, pink shirt and clothes neatly folded. On the quilt I admire his profile. Looking at the ceiling I am free and make secret faces at the events of 'before'. With my legs I enjoy the space I have.

'You look really happy, you do. I wasn't expecting you to be like this, you know.'

The next client is lying on the bed. His eyes are on me, on my body. He comes in a self-contained sort of way. He doesn't like my seeing it. He looks mean, nervy, brooding. He puts his clothes on and circles me. I try to remember if I should remember him.

'Er . . . do you want a smoke? It's good dope.'

'No, thanks.'

'D'you mind if I have a smoke here?'

'No, that's OK.'

He sits down on a sofa. I watch his pleasantly rounded fingers working on the cigarette. He lifts a can of beer from a denim bag. He cracks open the can and caresses it. I look at the shiny hardness of the words on the can. Heavily he sucks some of the beer and puts the

can on the carpet. The can is another alien in the room.
With exaggerated solemnity he lights the joint. He sucks
even more heavily on that and covers the room, then
me, with his eyes.

'What are you doing this for, then?'

'It's what I want to do.'

'Well, of course, if you wanna get laid, there's that, I
suppose.'

'That's not what I mean.' But I don't need him to
know what I mean.

'If I was a woman that's what I'd do. I envy you.'

I watch the ash fall on his jeans, and all the other
stains on his jeans.

'It's wrong, you know, what you do.'

'Why?'

'You lure, you entice men, it's harmful.'

He sucks and sucks on the joint and it fills and
contorts his face. I can smell the fumes and the beer. I
remember smoking dope so as not to upset people. I'm
glad I can get rid of it now.

'What do you do for a living?'

'I bake bread.'

'Well, white bread isn't good for people.'

The face behind the smoke. I like looking at his gentle
childlike fingernails.

'It must be awful for you to go on being here with
that fucking phone ringing. I can't stand phones ringing. Yeah, it's all right for you. I wish I was a woman.
What makes you tick? I wanna know why you're doing
this. You must have had psychiatric treatment. That's
the reason you do it.'

'No.'

'Yeah, I've got two kids to look after. My wife's in a
mental hospital.'

I feel sorry for both of them.

'So there must be something wrong with you to do this. It's degrading, that's what it is.'

His nails look younger than he does. I look at myself listening to his untrue words.

At last he's gone. I remove the joint and can before they change the room. I listen for silence in the house and take the rubbish through the dark hall and into the waterlogged dustbin. My hair gets moist and fluffy. There's rush-hour activity around. From the sour darkness I open the door to the room and see it anew, fresh.

Under *Cosmopolitan* I've hidden the library book. I turn on *Crossroads*. I flick through *Paradise Papers*. It's about matriarchy and goddess worship. I smell the expensive colourful smell of *Cosmopolitan* and Meg Mortimer appears at her desk. I remember watching her the first time, when I had a place to live, minding Arab-Portuguese children for £4 for two weeks till I left exhausted. She was a fearful threat to me. She had the energy to run a motel. Now I try to unmask her. I alight on a passage in the book about what were described by historians as temple prostitutes. They weren't prostitutes at all, they were involved in ritual worship. On the screen Sandy is zooming round in his wheelchair. I'm glad I'm not Irma Kurtz. I flick through bodies enshrouded in rich red and mauve coats on lovely-smelling paper.

I go to Hamley's for Bill's and Ben's Christmas presents. Through the bus windows I absorb streetlights through the raindrops.

At Blodminster we have our Christmas at a different time. I wait with Ben for a train. I buy him two small cans of lemonade. When he has drunk a little, he has fun pouring them into each other. Then I see a guy opposite. He hasn't enough clothes to keep out the cold. He looks anxiously for dregs of tea and often walks up to an open train for the warmth he can get. He is not seen by the others in the waiting room. Ben's enjoyment is torture to him.

'Why did you give money to that man?' asks Ben.

As most nights, when I go to sleep I think through the layers and layers of people in the world and try to get through them so I can feel alone.

Christmas Day, Boxing Day, I fast and listen to a quiet London.

'Did you enjoy the holiday?'

'Yes, thank you,' as I enclose him in rubber.

It's my first New Year.

Phone purring, buzzer buzzing, clients coming, my legs linking necks, crucifixes hitting my cunt, and I shut my eyes in comfort. 'Fun and drama, life and dreams,' sings Capital Radio. My thoughts turn to the past and Gideon. I see now the words he said and hear his meanings. I start to fill the silence I gave him with words of my own. Eventually Gideon moved to Sydney, went to a psychiatrist because I wouldn't marry him. He wanted me to see his psychiatrist to help me change my mind. I thought I might find out about my eating problem. I didn't. They asked about my sex life, which they liked, but I already knew about that.

Outside I feel exquisite, walking along the road and feeling the air on me. People outside seem nice, too. Then I stop working for a while and read magazines: the *Leveller* and *Seed*. And I look at and observe what sex is like for others.

In the mirror an entwined client is bending over me and massaging my breasts. I look at his reflected body.

It is far enough away from me. I look at me. I choose the rules. I answer the phone and make appointments from late morning till early evening, Monday to Friday. And when I've had enough I listen to the silence and the radio and go out and look at everything. Wake up smoothly, deliciously, happily in the late morning. The day will belong to me – it is my own, unmolested day. Listen to a phone-in while washing and then Capital for clients' ears.

Afterwards, washing and creaming my hands, I remember Jackanory asking me to write lists of what I liked doing. When he saw it he said, 'It's not quite what I meant. I was trying to find out what sort of job you'd like.' There were items like 'stroking my body with cream and oil', 'not being frightened', 'listening to the sea'.

I look at the swirling patterns on the mantelpiece. While I rub some buttocks with ice, brought in a Tesco bag, while a client tightens pearls around his balls and my neck, through cuddles and gasps and groans, the patterns multiply. And, as all manner of limbs pass between my thighs, I feel my body becoming more stable than ever before.

Walking in my outside clothes in central London, I hate the angles, the staleness, the grime around me, but inside I never lose what started when I began self-hypnosis. Down Baker Street, a guy is making silly noises at me. He gets abreast of me and the noises become more irritating. I look unhearing and do a right turn straight at him. He disappears.

Every Thursday afternoon I watch the washing whirling round and washed clean at the launderette, read *Time Out* and avoid the manager, if he's there. Every Friday, I clean the room. Saturday I run through the

smoky glass doors of the building society just before
noon, before the black-uniformed men lock it. Then a
special treat, a meal at the Rowan Tree or another
vegetarian restaurant, and take-away food for the evening meal. Explore shops and crowds in Oxford Street,
Kensington High Street and Kensington Market, look at
things I can have, then a bus back to Peachy Hill and
climb up the hill laden with cartons of fruit juice to
prepare for Sunday's fast. Wash my hair while the radio
encourages me to 'get out and enjoy yourself'. I escape
from a touch of guilt for doing what I've wanted to do.
Before, there were always people telling me what I
wanted to do.

Washed, showered, I slip into my sleeping bag, eat
my meal and watch telly. I eat from the take-away
carton, and eating is becoming unfearful and whole-
some. I'm learning to control the cravings I had. The
room is bare of stored food and domesticity and I can
afford to eat beautiful food. When I can't control my
appetite, it is mostly good food I eat. I use only the few
items of crockery and cutlery left by the Patels, and the
transparent cup and saucer I drink herb tea from. At a
house I worked in for three weeks, they had a dish-
washer. They had to have hoards of unnecessary ugly
crockery to fill it. They were dressed up to the nines
from 7.30 in the morning and so was the kitchen.

The room is almost free of personal things, yet when
I'm by myself there it is – my personal place.

Then I fast from food, people, money, clothes, telly,
till Monday. I empty myself of them all: the radio and
fruit juice and catching up with what happened to me
before. From my own branch, my own address, I look
at the past when I was always on other people's

branches. I start to see what I could, should have said and done.

For two and a half years in England I was married to Nodi. There was no heating, radio, newspapers, my body just felt fear and cold. Numb and blue from the knees down. When I got a red bonnet I felt my brain work enough to talk a bit. I was hardly strong enough to use the pointed tin opener, and when I got one that turned round it was lovely.

My husband and parents said they were middle-class but I didn't know what they meant. He was a teacher and thought he was intelligent and talked about being intelligent. I tried to believe that he and the kids had something to do with me but I couldn't. No one else believed they were my husband and kids either. I didn't notice furniture then, didn't know what it meant or what decorating a place was. I knew some time I'd find people I could talk to and whom I wanted to be with. After the second child was born, my mother-in-law gave me a radio, but I didn't know how to listen to it yet. On the way to Australia by ship, Tahiti was a place I could have stayed, dancing in the open-air nightclub there with a Tahitian guy. Nearing Australia I followed people on deck who were catching the first sounds from Australia on their transistors. Nodi appeared and threw my radio into the Pacific Ocean. Australia felt like home. Nodi went into hospital for alcoholism; Paul, my neighbour, gave me my first avocado pear, and we had sex.

Now I read a book about a starving woman in Brazil. She has a radio.

Monday. I feel my insides rested and clean and taste red grape juice. Some nicotined lips pass by.

On Blodminster weekends with Bill and Ben, we listen to juke-boxes and play in amusement arcades. At a restaurant I sit too close to a man eating liver. It's gruesome. On a late Sunday-night walk up Peachy Hill I feel a brief panic that the house might be destroyed, might not be there, but it always is. And entering the hall I get a picture of what others might think of it. Then I unlock the room and see what it is for me. After Blodminster, Monday is a fast day.

Four sticks of jasmine incense are puffing away, and a client is completing his layers and layers of brown and grey woolly padding. I want to take away his king-size filter-tip cigarette and get back to *Seed*. Meanwhile we chat about phone-ins.

A tense client who becomes a little less tense but maybe never relaxes. He looks edgily around the room.

'What made you go into this, eh?'

'It's what I wanted to do.'

He twitches his hands.

'Huh. I can't believe that. I mean, I can understand a girl having an ambition to become a secretary or working in a shop, but this? No way.'

He gives a final twitch and leaves. I clear away his rubbish, wash hands, brush hair in mirror. Lying on my tummy on the bed, looking at *Seed* and stroking my skin against the quilt, I drink pear juice and try to imagine anyone wanting another job.

When I'm ready, I uncover the phone, change the station from a phone-in to Capital for clients.

'Is it personal?'

'Is it private?'

'Is it safe?'

In my jeans I tread on the grey-green pavement and see the grey-green buds up above. The evenings are lighter and whiter. It is spring but it is not my spring yet.

Amid all the smells of a cuddle I think of my reactions

to a story on the last phone-in. A guy of nineteen had rung in, talking of how he was caring for his two babies as a hard-up single parent. My heart had gone out to him, wanting to send him things and to help him. But I wouldn't have felt like that if it had been a girl. Interesting. I start to consider: that was impartial, that was a good thing. I delve into that experience and trace patterns on the ceiling with my toes.

'I guess they're just in and out, most of them. It must be boring. I wanna please you.'

When he comes I'm held in his entrapping arms for many seconds till I free myself without seeming to.

'You look happy,' he says suspiciously.

9
The Green Apple

Outside, it is a grey, late spring day. I lie on the floor and do self-hypnosis. I go very deep till I can't feel the floor. My body melts, the beach is vivid and brilliant. I can feel the coarse, bleached sand and the smooth rocks against my body. I come to, and enjoy my recreated self. I am fascinated and delighted at acting in a vacuum. What is it, my job? I can make it anything I like. I don't know anyone else doing it. What others might do is a mystery. I'm far, far away from them, only connected by snippets of words I pick up from clients, from the phone, 'French', 'Greek', 'Swedish'. I could be doing anything, that's the greatest freedom.

It's dark out. I wash my face and put apricot and avocado lotion on it. A new phone-in programme. David Simmons. He sounds pissed off. He says, 'I feel like a cabbage today. I just want cabbage calls.'

Buzzer sounds, switch to Capital. 'In tune with London, yeh, yeh, yeh.'

Shake hair around, check room. It's OK, no signs of my personal life. I open the door on a face, faces that may or may not be clients. We look, I smile, they smile, till I know they're not TV repair men, Jehovah's Witnesses or people who say they're coming to collect their mail. Little looks and, when we both know, they follow me into the house. The feeling that I might get bopped on the head before I start livens up the drab hall. In that moment I know I don't want to be anyone else in the world.

They are safely in the room. I stand still while shoes and boots prowl the carpet. They hand over their notes purposefully, happily, unbelievingly, significantly, coyly, flirtatiously, importantly – sometimes as if they don't want to lose connection with them. I make the money and the owner's world disappear, put it where it can be scented and flavoured with honey, cinnamon and herb teas.

Like strange parcels, their layers of clothes are unwrapped. Would I ever be with people wearing these? Their clothes are foreign to this room. Sometimes my clothes touch theirs as they're tossed on a chair, or my pants touch their shoes, but I don't really believe it. Without their clothes they are not aliens in the room. Skin on skin on silky sheets, white on white on pink, white on olive on pink, white on brown on mauve, white on black on mauve, white on white on mauve.

Evenings getting lighter, should get some summer soon, and their armpits are wetter. I train myself to avoid personal pleasure and in the dance of exploration I start to consider, and there's not much to consider, so I think back. All the words that were used. The words I saw but didn't understand. With Jed I first used 'constructive' and knew what it meant. And now I start to hear and understand people from the time when I understood nothing but sex.

I focus on different parts of my body and they become stronger. Some legs are more like mine than I'd like them to be – can legs be female or male? And my naked toenails and their naked toenails look alike. But in the ceremony I am different and they are different. I trace my fingers along spine after spine after spine. I imagine being a flat white fish fried in a pan till I am scrunchy soft and how it must feel to have my spine hooked up by a huge fork and eased out of my bodily flesh. I marvel at random hues and patterns on random bodies, bright red pubic hair, a body creamy and bald of hair from head to toe. My honey-flavoured lips numb on aftershaved pricks. My herb-tea breath takes in strange meals which rise from all their pores. Cheesecake, Opal mints, fruit gums, peppermint chewing gum, Marlboro, jam pudding, Gauloises, cough mixture, No. 10, stew, coffee, brandy – I breathe them in and breathe them out. And bones dig into me from strange angles. Will they ever hurt me or damage me? I go limp and learn to preserve my body. Moans and sighs break like waves over my skin. Myriads of eyes focus on me as if I'm something other.

Sometimes the eyes look into mine and try to merge. I shut my eyes. And I know that here I am at home, whatever heavy metalware may crash across my cunt and my eyes. I say goodbye as they reclothe themselves for their world. I shut the door smiling, purified. Then I emerge into new daylight. At night I take my working sheets off the bed and lie down to sleep in my private sleeping bag.

At Selfridges I go through the clothes with labels and prices on them. I find enormous brilliant flowers made of dyed birds' feathers. I hand over notes and receive coins, not listening to or looking at the price. I stand among the dull-coloured crowd with my bunch of flowers and stroke them against my face. A vivid-faced man is looking at me out of the corners of his eyes. I turn and mingle in the crowd. He's still there watching.

I'm back in the room. In the round mirror the top finger phalanges are olive Mediterranean mauve and are taking bits of clothing off me. The nub of his prick should match his fingers. It does. I watch us entwining and the mirror gleams.

I dispose of his tissue-covered rubber containing hot liquid, wash hands, shake hair, switch on *Crossroads* and read about different types of finger phalanges which signify mental, spiritual or physical planes. Another book divides handwriting into round, triangular, square, and squiggly – loving, sexy, materialistic and artistic. Meg and Sandy have a heart-to-heart.

Next afternoon, I go to the launderette. I put coins in the machine, it clicks and the cycle starts, and the coins come back to me. If I use the same machine I get a free wash every time I go there. I sit and watch the kaleidoscope of clothes turn and flop. I watch the strangely shaped women in clothes I wouldn't wear and feel myself into their bodies. The manager comes in occasionally to empty the machines.

'I'd like to be your sugar daddy,' he says. 'I'd treat you well. You're such a sweet girl.'

Does he know what I'm doing? No. This is the outside world where no one knows that at all.

'No, thank you.' I disappear with *Time Out* and eat an avocado pear behind it.

In the room I look at my toes skating across the ceiling. The client has put a beautiful, glossy, mauve cigarette packet and gold lighting equipment on the mantelpiece. As his back heaves, I catch glimpses of the pretty packet and lighter. Once I thought I needed such things and wanted them. Now that I can afford to, I know I don't. I muse on this while he comes.

On telly there's a comedy show – an Indian guy dressed in conventional English clothes arrives home and takes them off to reveal floppy trousers. Next day

an Indian client comes in dressed in conventional English clothes and underneath he's the same as the one on
telly.

A beautiful asymmetric and metallic Star of David and
floppy hair tickle my cunt and I look at the pretty
patterns on the ceiling. A metal speculum is warmed in
hot water and inserted. The lamps and the ceiling are
different. It's my check-up at a new special clinic. I look
at everyone attending me and watch them working. A
different environment. How different is it? I wonder.
Novelty of sitting clothed at a diagonal angle to the
desk. I take my time answering questions and take my
time listening to them. I'm clean and uninfected, I'm
told. I'm always that, now.

In the middle of the week, Anna Raeburn, Adrian
Love and the Doctor talk of 'personal, sexual and
emotional problems'. It seems strange, people talking
about things that I've only done. It seems a different
thing altogether. 'There are three places in London I
can send you for psychosexual counselling,' says Anna
Raeburn. 'Your hang-ups.' 'Their hang-ups.' 'My relationship.' 'His relationship.' 'Bollocks,' shouts Anna.
Adrian jingles and the Doctor chimes in.

I dispose of the last rubber in a polythene bag, wash
my hands, brush my hair, massage myself with wheat-
germ lotion. I sit cross-legged on the bed after an
afternoon of sucking rubbered cocks and reading about
finger phalanges. On the news there are more bomb
scares, bomb warnings. I look at the feathered flowers.

Voices come through from the phone.

'How much?'

'How big?'

'How small?'

'Is it safe?'

'Where do you come from?'

'What do you do?'

'What colour?'

'What shape?'

'Do you enjoy it?'

'Do you like it?'

'Is it complete?'

'You sound very young.'

'Prostitute!'

'VD, VD, VD, VD, VD, VD, VD.'

'Remember me, I'm John, I came ten days ago, it was so nice, can I come this afternoon?'

'Is that the Nat West Bank?'

Telephone voices whirling. I make my voice sound older and posher. It could be the police. It could be the landlord checking up on me or getting someone else to. It could be people I've known who don't know it's me, or do they? It could be anyone. It is anyone.

'When?'

'Where?'

'I don't want to let you down.'

'Am I too old?'

'Am I too young?'

'I'm stuck in a traffic jam.'

I put a cushion over the phone.

I'm curled up with the phone, my mirror, mildly-smelling *Cosmopolitan*, non-smelling *Spare Rib*, smooth-smelling *Small Boats*. *General Hospital* on telly. A book about childhood through the centuries says the idea of childhood didn't really exist till quite recently. In the country till I was seven I remember feeding the cows in the field next door – the feel of the bullock's tongue on my hands, like the man's jaw the first time I was kissed.

At four I had a sort of vision of dancing and healing all the people I knew who were sick, in the hall at the village school. At seven, after we'd moved into the town, I knew I didn't belong in the world of my parents, brother and sister, a bit closer to friends, but one day I'd be somewhere I belonged.

I make mysterious entrances through the hall with clients. When the buzzer goes, I hide magazines and walk stealthily to the front door, hoping no one else is around. But it's all right, mostly couples live here and, if I ever come across anyone, the women pretend not to see me because of the men and the men pretend not to see me because of the women. My fantasy is real. I'm in peace.

Outside a guy is carrying a too heavy case up a hill. I help him and then disappear before he can talk to me. And inside the room:

'That's nice.'

'That's good.'

'You're sweet.'

'You're lovely.'

'What you doing this for?'

'It must be degrading.'

'It must be boring.'

'Tell me if you don't like anything I do.'

'Aren't you scared?'

'I mean, I'm all right, I work in a hospital.'

'I'd do it if I were a woman.'

'It can't be very nice for you.'

'I bet most of them are just in and out.'

'I want you to enjoy it.'

'Am I the first?'

'Am I the last?'

'I've never done this before.'

'I didn't know what to expect.'

'I don't like to see you doing this.'

'I've just come from the desert.'

'I'm on a dope charge. I reckon I'll get six months. This is to see me through it.'

'We're like old friends.'

'This is a nice place you've got here.'

'With the money you earn, surely you can afford somewhere more salubrious?'

'Oh, I envy women, wearing loose clothing in this weather,' as they struggle with the angles of their clothes. And I smile and wash my hands and feel my voice grow stronger when I speak. 'And I'll miss you . . . I don't wanna let you go.'

I've been here longer than anywhere. It is my place now. And I'm talking to grown-ups now.

'Heavily congested at the Hammersmith flyover.'

'Capital 194.'

My music is on. As the clients come and come, I listen to some of what they say and examine their words. I let cutting words from the past empty and explode, and I get rid of them. So the reality of this room is what I have. In the past I don't think it was me at all.

On telly a tight-mouthed MP is trying to make abortions harder to get. There's to be a demo. It won't break any of the rules to go.

Outside I renew my cards, which are fading quickly in the new summer sun. In Regent's Park I sit on the grass. I look at the light on the leaves. I write to Gideon and tell him what I would have felt if it had really been me there with him. I remember being a love object to him and having no feelings and watching him go on about how he felt about me. I didn't know what to do.

During the night phone-ins, voices from all over London.

'Disgusting', 'shouldn't be allowed', 'my problem', 'what I think is . . .', 'the problems of loneliness', 'the problems of the young', 'the problems of the old', 'the problems of the handicapped', 'the problems of terrorism'. The host is surrounded by these voices. Sometimes they make me angry but he's never angry. That comforts me. There's no need for people to hurt me with their words any more. Now I can listen to them. And when I turn the radio and the telly off and close the door on clients, I can bask and listen to my silence.

Depositing tied-up polythene bags of rubbers and tissues in the bin in the back garden, I pass another tenant who doesn't look at me. In the room I'm waiting for a client to leave. He hovers.

'I'd like to see you again.'

'Yes, fine.'

'I mean, I'd like to take you out to dinner. Surely you'd like that, then there'd be no rush. We could enjoy ourselves.'

I'm amazed. How could he imagine I could do that? How could I have such intimacy with him? I couldn't even walk down the road with him. I only want to walk by myself till I'm ready.

In *Spare Rib* I learn the laws on prostitution. What I'm doing is quite legal. If another girl was working with me, it wouldn't be. That's lovely, I only want to work alone. If a guy was living with me where I work, he could be done for 'living off immoral earnings'. My dream comes true. And the law protects my dream of privacy. This must be why Pyrrhus has kept clear of me. I've wanted to live this way for so long. Soliciting in the street is illegal. I couldn't do that because outside

I don't work. Outside I couldn't be Dawn. People don't bump into me on the streets the way they used to.

'Your room is small?'

'Your room is big?'

They touch me and fall off like pretty drops of water.

Next Monday is a bank holiday.

'What are you doing for the holiday, then? Are you going away?'

'Oh yes, I'm going into the country.' It seems to be a suitable reply. They tell me all their bank-holiday problems.

I wash, clean the room, wash my hair, shower, buy fruit juice, get magazines, fast on fruit juice, rest, think and am till the holiday stops.

'Did you have a good holiday? What did you do?'

'Yes.'

'What did you do? I bet you had some parties. You look as if you've enjoyed yourself.'

'Yes, I had some good parties.' We smile securely. And I'm back in the comfort of the only routine I've ever known, which I've known and made. Herbal tea, honey, orgasms, breaths and sighs float loosely round my white skin and my new silver-coloured watch gives nominal time when time is necessary.

It's the day of the demo. I wander around looking at the banners. Gays in long skirts, well, it's sensible for men to wear skirts. We start moving. I tell the woman next to me, 'When I was trying to get an abortion this guy, he was a major, he said, "It's a terrible thing to take life. Soldiers always abhor killing," but I heard him boast and tell great stories about hacking the Mau-Mau.' Brilliant yellow sun. At a snack bar at Marble Arch, I ask for a glass of brilliant yellow fizzy stuff. The guy pours it slowly, talks slowly and looks at my breasts slowly. I take the drink. With my back towards him I turn my head round, watching him as I drink.

In Blodminster at the fairground, with Ben. I take the kids out separately now because they like different things. No one knows I'm his parent so my privacy here is preserved too. I don't think I'd fancy being a full-time parent. It's a possibility, I suppose. At the dodgems, a guy straps us in. 'Is he your brother?'

'Yes.' I think, no, he's my great-aunt . . .

The big dipper. Ben leaves his chip packet and I leave a used *Cosmopolitan*. I shut my eyes, listen to the rock and roll and wonder what will happen to me. When it's over, I open my eyes. A black guy in purple leather is unstrapping us. He's looking through the *Cosmopolitan* and through me.

'Come back and have another ride. It'll be free. I'm off soon. I'll take you somewhere.'

He's reading the 'sensuality quiz', which I've filled in. Of course he doesn't know. Earlier I would have been with him or someone like him. Now in my happy social celibacy, I wonder what sex for pleasure will be like when I want it. And whom shall I want to have it with?

We go on a fast and violent roundabout. The strap of my handbag is hooked over my knee. It might be jolted away from me and someone could pinch it. That gives excitement to the rock and roll. Like leaving clients' notes on the mantelpiece occasionally, where they could pinch them and I couldn't stop them.

Back at Peachy Hill. The weight of my body is now a fairly stable nine stone. The clients' bodies in relation to it seem larger, smaller, fatter, thinner, heavier, lighter. The bodies change and mine does not. Notes handed

neatly and martially. Notes handed crumpled and
freely. Smooth notes from a cash machine. Sometimes
they are part of the clients, sometimes very separate.

Outside, people who may be neighbours give me
hard stares but they don't touch me. I wonder who they
are. Police cars make me nervous, but they are after
bombers, not me.

The leaves are bright with sunlight. I buy capsicums.
There is lightning, a storm breaks, a real thunderstorm.
Everyone is sheltering in shops and doorways. The
water beats down on me and the paper bag dissolves. I
soak my clothes and my body in the rain, holding two
shining clean capsicums.

After the storm I enjoy the light on the trees, the light
on people's skins. More people are beautiful to me now
than I ever believed possible. With clients I am
detached, but in a sense I feel very close to them. I stop
hating London and start to love . . .

A transparent stain on the sheet. I toss last week's *Time
Out* over it, and read this week's. I read Film, words
and photos, Theatre, just photos, skip Music and get to
Miscellaneous.

Buzzer goes loud and long and a knock on the door.
Not a client. It's a policeman. I try to look ordinary.

'Does a John Smith live here?'

'No, I don't think so.'

'Well, he may be using a false name.'

I look blank while I think. 'Oh.'

He looks at my tits and I remain blank.

'Well, if you get any joy, let us know.' He gives me
his name and phone number.

He rings up a few times saying, 'Any joy?' and I say,
'No.' I find joy hard to associate with a policeman.

'This bed's too soft, let's go on the floor.'

I feel myself being pulverized against the floor. I think of the word 'grind'. I see myself becoming dust. If he's like this in sex, what would he be like if he were trying to hurt me? My thoughts skip and drift off. Maybe he puts more energy into sex, and doesn't want to hurt people.

'How'd you like us to spend the night together?'

'No, I don't spend nights.'

They give reasons.

'I've bust up with my girlfriend.' 'I'm a writer.' 'I've just been to Leeds.'

'Is that a colour telly?'

'No.'

'Why not? You should have a colour telly with the money you make.'

'Oh.' I don't want a colour telly.

'Is that your Mini outside?'

'No.'

'The blue Volvo, then?'

'No.' I don't know the names, though sometimes I notice the colours of cars.

'Well, which is your car?'

'I don't have a car.'

'You don't have a *car*! Why ever not? When are you going to get one?'

'I don't want a car.'

Shock, horror.

'But you must want a car!'

A client comes along hot from his car seat. He touches and starts to turn my nipple. I can feel he's more used to touching and turning the ignition or whatever turns cars on than touching real flesh. Imagine touching cars and things more than people, to know things rather than people. I feel sorry for him. I never let clients touch my nipples after that.

In Oxford Street, I look at people whose job isn't sex. Do they become distorted by what they handle day after day? Relentlessly, they handle money, coins, clothes, bags, food, metal, implements, crockery. I wander among the clothes, sometimes in time to the music, circling people and racks of clothes. I stroke a fur coat.

In the Rowan Tree I look at a wholemeal apple pie and a pale guy hovers behind it. Memory of a girl I knew making an apple pie. I sat and watched the way she looked as if she had done it many times before, and envied her being used to something. For me, everything was always unexpected. I resist the apple pie, get grape juice and sit down. The juice tastes as if I've never had it before. Everything is new to me.

In a self-service store, I buy matches from an Indian woman in a sari. She is trapped in the checkout with jewellery and heavy fingernails, metal cash register, cigarettes, tobacco, wooden jewellery hanging above her head. Her hair is cut in discord with the sari. But her face is still beautiful.

At the zebra crossing, a guy with a grey suit and glasses is hunched behind the driving wheel of a car. In the past I would have judged him as unattractive. Now I know that beneath all the clothes he could be sweet and gentle.

A client eases himself out of me.

'What would you do if someone died like this?'

'What?'

'Yeah, there was a story I heard. Some old guy in France and the rigor mortis set in.'

'Well, I'd have to be asleep.' We laugh. 'Rigor mortis takes a little while, I think.'

A client with smooth black hair.

'Do you like this? I want to please you. I want you to enjoy it. Is it good? Am I doing what you like?'

I wonder how it would be to have real sex with him.

I connect with my phone.

'Am I the first?'

'Am I the last?'

'How much do you make?'

'How many a day?'

'I know you now, we're like old friends.'

'My regular afternoon.'

'God bless.' Kiss on the cheek.

'It's good in 'ere, innit?'

And I dissuade the ones who want to come along too regularly, so no one can become familiar in my life, so no one person stands out. They must all be equal. Time flows smoothly while I'm working.

Dispose of rubbish, wash hands, wash hair, stretch out, turn from Capital to David Simmons's phone-in. Read about astrology, fingerprints, women in Greece – even slaves had the right to expose babies on the hillsides.

David Simmons says, 'What would you do if the world was going to end in thirty minutes and there was nothing you could do about it?'

Buzzer rings, switch off '194, in tune with London'. A pink-faced and pink-cocked guy who's been here before and said that he was a virgin, is bringing a pile of magazines from Germany.

'Do you want to buy them? They're good value, you know.'

So I flick through them and think it might be a good

investment. There's a merry Alsatian enjoying himself with a bored model. He finishes. I put the mags in the cupboard, next to the Co-op stamps. Now I've got three types of literature: *Cosmopolitan*, *Private Eye*, etc., which can always be on view; porn mags only if asked for; *Spare Rib*, *Seed*, the *Leveller*, library books when the room is just for me.

I lick rubber over his cock.

I wonder what I'd do if the world was going to end in thirty minutes? I think I'd sit and happily meditate on my life, or I could go and smash glass in cars and buildings, that'd be nice too. He finishes.

Buzzings, beepings, comings, goings, buffings, puffings, unbelievable angles, bodies. I skim the silky sheets and get a craving to have clothes on for a while and go outside.

Denim on my legs, wind on my face and swirling my pink coat. Green leaves start to float to the ground.

On a grey velvet chair in Sacha's in Oxford Street, a guy pulls a soft leather boot up my leg and zips it up delicately, like me slowly putting a rubber on a client. I look at his pale podgy hands and head against the creamy leather.

'Cash or cheque?'

'Oh, cash.' I wouldn't like to have a chequebook.

At a photo booth I brush my hair and take four photos. I keep my face blank, to see it naked. A guy in a check suit is waiting for photos. He chats. He needs them to be a mercenary in Africa. I avoid him, get my photos and flap them in the wind. Pass into the tube with black bomb warnings on either side. Someone is being carried out on a stretcher. Has it happened? Is it a bomb? No, it's just an ill person, I think.

Back in the room one leg draws designs on the ceiling.

The other is ground on pink silkiness. Perhaps here is where most people are at their most beautiful, their most human. I eat an avocado and find my last photos, taken in a booth on the way from Jed's to meeting Cyrrhus the landlord. I look at the frightened smile. In my new photos I look happier even though I'm not smiling.

Cosmopolitan open at the problem page. How can people have problem-page problems about sex? For me, there was always sex, before it had a name or words to spoil it. It just belonged to me and I to it. I rub avocado on my skin, and look at the *TV Times* horoscope.

Phone purrs.

'Do you enjoy it?'

Buzzer goes.

'You look as if you enjoy it.'

'You seem peaceful here.'

They think that I am with them. Drops of water in an ocean. They don't know what I'm enjoying. What they 'are' doesn't touch me. Sometimes I see what I would think of them outside. Then I see my likes and dislikes. I train myself and float into another realm.

A client is licking me. I've accidentally read about torture in *Time Out*. I feel the pain in my body but not for days after, as I used to. As a three-year-old I had a diphtheria jab, and when my baby sister had hers I cried with her pain. Saw only four films before I was eighteen. Someone was burned in each one. I felt their pain years after. Here there are happy smiling faces on the pillows. Now I feel other people's pleasure, there's no pain.

A client who looks as if he's been up a chimney. He has about a quarter of an inch of dirt in his fingernails.

I let him put some of it up my cunt. I know he can't make me dirty now.

From the cupboard I take my drawing book from years ago. I turn to a new page and open my tin of oil pastels. I do what I feel. I do one complete apple. That's what I am and around me is free space. Flick through previous pages where I was a pink and white egglike creature, sometimes with drops of blood inside, crushed and hemmed in by other shapes.

10

The Cricklewood Bell Snatcher

A very quiet day. The phone rings and there are many silences on it. No one comes round for any of the appointments that have been made. I paint nail polish stars on the telephone.

A ballpoint taps on the window.

'Is your bell working?'

We look at it. The flex has been cut in half.

He mounts me in front of the mirror and I flick a silver belt across him every now and then. Afterwards he fixes the flex for me.

I continue to paint the phone with sparkly pink nail polish – a custom telephone.

'I bet you get some guys that you don't want along. What do you do if they're Irish or coloured or something?'

I look at him, surprised. Then I look at him again and think that in the past my prejudice would have cancelled him out. Now I'm in another realm. A naked penis is placed on a chair for my bare feet to tread on. Outside with my new creamy boots I tread the dust and fallen leaves. The only danger is when they are about to come on top of me. Which way will their heads go down? I flick the right way to avoid the head hitting mine.

In the Rowan Tree I sit secure and untouched. In shops people listen to me. I can chat to them. I'm happy outside, too. On the phone and with clients, I can hear the sound of my voice. I remember when no one could hear me and I had nothing to say.

On Saturday evening I'm washing my hair and listening to the radio. A voice very close to the window shouts, 'Fucking prostitute!' I listen to the words, then lose them. I climb into my sleeping bag, eat salad and prepare for my Sunday fast and quiet time.

Sunday – music, no telly, the weather is dull outside. I remain here till I start work on Monday.

From my cocoon I look at the misty intricate patterns of the curtains. I float with them into my past and make it into a pattern. Through the curtains, a black tree hard and delicate against a nothing sky. The shape of my earlier life changes. Events I believed big shrink so I can hardly see them. What I thought was small enlarges to its full size. Things I never saw, I see and experience now. If I had really been there, then I could have directed my life.

Sunday night the buzzer wakens me. What is it at this time? I open the front door an inch and peep out. Three guys run nervously laughing to their car.

Monday and a client puts notes on the mantelpiece. I put the beach stone on them. I enclose him, swirl around him and smile at the ceiling.

'What about your conscience?'

'Pardon?'

'How do you feel about what you do? I'm concerned. It can't be good for you.'

'I'm fine, thank you.' He can pick the notes up and run but I don't think he will. I'm lucky. He comes back next day and offers me a flat and work. I decline.

I suck a rubbered aftershaved cock and meditate on men from my life before. Y was nothing, I wasn't with him. I was a love object. U was sexy in a personal way.

Q was an interesting guy to know. T was oppressed
and might be dead. S was the first person I had feelings
for. That was important. R told me what I thought, felt
and knew, when I didn't think, feel or know anything.

I'm underneath a Brut-smelling armpit. Curry kisses,
processed-peas kisses, coffee kisses.

I listen to the radio and massage a pair of meaty
buttocks like Mr Kitten's but a different colour. He turns
over. I start stroking him.

'What did you do before this?'

'I worked in a massage parlour.'

'Oh, where?'

'Copplestone Mews.'

'Oh yeah, I went there.'

'Who was there when you were there? An Italian
girl?' I think of Gemma.

'No, I don't think so. There was a girl with a big
bruise on her leg and a purple see-through shirt.'

I listen to him describe me then. Me now is someone
he's meeting for the first time. I remember the bruise.
Remember peeing in the wash basin because the loo in
the corridor was too cold. I fell off the basin and bruised
my leg on the massage table. I remember the eternal
cold of my life before. Now I can make the winters
warm.

My hair is all around my face as with my tongue I
introduce a cock to his rubber and lick it on him. I
sprawl over and investigate the craters of his trunk. He
puts my hair behind my ears so he can see more of me
but it curtains my face again. I consider his freckles and
taste the rubber. The bits of bodies that people don't
count as beautiful. I think of all the words people put
on me before. I flick my beads over his chest and

quivering stomach. I lift them up and lift some of their
words off my life. I start to see it as it was.

It's black outside and I drift over smooth, warm skin.
I look at coarse, black hair coming out of the palest skin,
skin so transparent that the hair roots show beneath it.
I wonder at the roughness and delicacy. Then there is
hammering at me on the silk bed. I avoid damage and
listen to the free stillness inside me. Phone-in voices
waft in from the dark outside. In the pink light I stroke
dark mouse-coloured balls.

When it's time I turn off the radio, muffle the phone,
wash my hands and brush my hair and sit and feel the
silence. I let it touch me all around and I feed on it.

Next day is quiet. The phone rings a lot. I read *Private
Eye* and the book about children through the centuries
and another about women through the centuries. I can
read while speaking on the phone now. No one comes
around.

I go out to take the library books back. In the hall I
see the bell has been cut again. The front door is slightly
open. Who is doing it? Someone from outside or inside?
I'm scared, it might stop everything. My life might stop.
At the library I wander around the different letters of
the alphabet. It's like a lucky dip. Will I catch something
I like? At the desk there are new barricades and black
bomb warnings. A woman with fantastically long heavy
hair picks up my books. The hair is bound and braided
round her head. There is so much of it, it seems a waste
to hide it in a library. She doesn't stamp my books, she
has a little bleeping instrument which she passes over
them as if searching them for something. She is very
grown up. She would have frightened me before. Now
I can admire her hair and think that even in an ugly job
there can be beautiful hair. She must search more books

than I do cocks. And she has to be on public display for
it.

As I go through the door at Peachy Rise, a client
who's been before comes in with me. I'm in my outside
clothes so I don't feel quite right. But, when I switch
the light on and take my clothes off, I become what I
want to be with him. He shows me how to fix the flex
of the bell. Then the light above the wash-basin mirror
goes.

An enormously fat guy says he's a butcher. He has a
smoked-pork smell. He puts notes on the mantelpiece
and rams the beach stone on top of them. I wonder
how I'll survive his weight but I make sure I'm only
under a third of it. He offers to fix the light. It's fiddly.
He uses my screwdriver and my small knife. It gets
tedious having him in the room for so long.

'I've nearly done it. Would you just have a look
outside to check there's no one around or cars parked
or anything? I don't want anyone to recognize me on
the way out. Thanks.'

After looking out I shut the front door behind me.
He's coming towards me. I let him go out of the door. I
check the mantelpiece. There's nothing under the beach
stone. He's charged me for fixing the light. It's funny.

A nervous client comes in. He has the smell of
someone who's never been dirty but has never washed
either.

'Look, I didn't want to do anything, now, but I just
wanted to ask you, could you do all I've written down?'
He takes a lined sheet of paper from his tweed jacket.
He has grime on his fingernails. My eyes skim over the
paper but I don't read the words. I'm not going to do
anything that's written down, it would spoil it. I act so
that he won't come back.

Sometimes for fun I agree to take a cheque. I learn to look at the signature and read from them whether they will bounce or not.

'It won't be long before the worst is over,' they say about the weather.

A client happily takes his shoes and socks off.

'I hate shoes,' he says. 'I've just come from a beach in South Africa. It's fantastic. You don't need anything on the beach.'

I warm to the idea of a beach. He has hazel eyes and fair hair. I splay myself around him on the bed. In the outside world I think I could do him unrubbered. I could fancy someone with fair hair. So there are more people I can like now in a personal way. I take his notes to the bank and try to find the quickest way to send it to Prince in the States.

'The quickest way would be if you knew his bank-account number. We could send it straight then.'

'He hasn't got one. He's in prison.'

The guy thinks bank accounts are part of being human.

In the street the weather is dingy, but the shops seem more colourful. I notice things I never did before, like red brick on buildings. There are more people to see and wonder at. Fruit on stands is shining and brilliant. I smell aftershaves, perfumes, cigarettes, and catch a whiff of a luxurious cigar. Car headlights shine on shop windows. Many men are standing studying a display of watches. I remember once, in the past, waiting for a bus in Oxford Street by this very shop, when watches and radios were so remote that people who had them seemed almost another species. Even tissues were a luxury. I wriggle my way through groups of men looking in the watch shop. I'm the only girl looking at the watches. The watches have all stopped at different times. The faces are beautiful and the prices seem to have nothing to do with them. I want to look for the perfect watch, find out which one I like best. A few months ago I was going to buy it when I'd found it, but now I won't. Once I've found it, all I need to do is come and look at it sometimes.

I go to the post office to send the money order to Prince. I pass supermarkets and shops selling take-away food. I remember when nearly every minute I had to stop food cravings, cravings for any kind of food, even food I didn't like. Now I walk past lots of food with hardly a twinge. In the Rowan Tree I choose lentil soup, wholemeal rolls and garlicky potato salad, and look through a book on witches, feeling civilized.

'So nice.'
　'So gentle.'
　'So calm.'
　'So lovely.'
　'So sweet.'
　'So tranquil.'
　'You're always so happy.'
　'I'm surprised.'
　'I'm amazed.'
　'What are you giggling at?'
　'I can't believe it.'
I cover skin with freckles, moles, warts, hairs curly and straight, tattoos, scars from operations and other things, smiling glances, contentment. I create neatness each time.

Tissues, rubbers, mucus, multiflavoured breath. On the phone strange ads are reported in places I've never been.

'I saw your ad in Notting Hill.'

'I don't advertise there.'

'Yeah, straight up. It said "dominatrix".'

On the phone I can always rely on the unexpected, and through the door, too.

A cock emerges from me coated with a wrinkled, bloodied rubber. A drop of blood falls on the apricot-coloured tissues. I make sure none of their accoutrements are left in the room. Each time I tidy and refresh the room, and each time I am refreshed, I am myself anew again and again. And when I feel the need for silence, I muffle the phone, ignore the buzzes of any extra clients and dive into silence. If need be, I can immerse myself in it for weeks.

The cold water gets colder, their hands get colder, my nipples get harder and their armpits drier. Christmas is coming.

A client is trembling on the bed afterwards instead of getting up as soon as I do.

'Do you mind if I just lie here for five minutes or so?'

'No, that's OK.'

I look at him lying there.

'I feel so guilty about this. I hate myself for coming here. You don't mind me being here a while?'

'No, it's OK.'

'Each time I come here I say I won't again, but I can't help it.'

He must have been before but I can't remember him. Depression oozes from him. I try not to let it touch me.

'I'm lonely. That's the matter. I don't know anyone here.'

I wonder how that can be a problem. I'm happy not knowing anyone.   * * *

'It's hard to meet people in London,' he says. 'It's all right for you, you're a lady.'

A Saturday. And I go to Kensington High Street. People in their clothes and people wanting clothes and lots of little objects in boxes. I look at a bag made of snakeskin and make a note of it in my notebook, in case I want to buy it. I look at coats in patchwork chamois leather. They feel nice to stroke. They are second-hand and the colour of bleached sand. I note them down too. I circle round and round till I've seen everything. Then I cross the road to an arcade of different clothes stalls.

A guy with weak blue eyes approaches me with a couple of coats on his arm. I smile and decline them. Another guy approaches me. I dodge the other way. Underneath a spotlight I see his face illuminated and the suggestion of little spots he used Valderma for. It's Claude Catsilk! I try to walk past, but it's no good, he knows I've recognized him.

'Amazing seeing you, amazing. I always knew somehow we'd see each other again. You look so well, quite different.'

He has a budding stall there. He shows me his till and the things he has acquired. We sit at the snack bar, neon-illuminated quiches under glass, and drink apple juice.

'This is what you should be drinking,' he said.

'I *do* drink it.'

He has a moustache, new rings and the clothes he wants. He wants me to go home with him. I watch the hands and eyes moving. He describes my coat and hair for a while.

'Do you have a boyfriend?'

'Sort of,' I say, to keep my distance.

'You're so modest. It's very clever. You're unconventional, like me,' he says. 'When can I see you?'

He writes his phone number for me. I don't give him mine.

'Well, not just yet.'

'When?'

'I'm not seeing anyone.'

'When?'

'I'm on a retreat. I'll call you when it's finished. When I've finished my retreat. In about a month.' As I leave, I look round me at things I might want.

Walking up Peachy Rise in the dusky afternoon, I see a dim figure hurrying from the house and going in the direction of the Cricklewood bus station. Something's happened. I get to the door. The bell has gone completely. He's taken it away! The Cricklewood Bell Snatcher! What does he want it for? Perhaps he's taken it to bed to wank with. I giggle to myself. In the garden raindrops hang in a beautiful pattern on the clothes line.

Next day there's a letter from Prince. He was out yesterday and is staying at his mother's, in Chicago. I'm glad for him. I don't think he'll write now so the last tie has gone. My life is really pure now. Except . . . Claude Catsilk is looming up. A shadow falls. I said I'd contact him in a month. I think about having to see him. Then I melt into self-hypnosis.

As I open my eyes again I see the room clearly. I feel the happiness in it. I can be happy. I don't have to do anything I don't want to or anything that isn't good for me. So I don't have to see anyone again till I want to, till I finish the retreat.

11
Afternoon Delight

'I'm a doctor,' he says, as he comes through the door.
  'Oh.'
  'I work at Shimmering Hospital part time. It's a really lovely hospital.'
  'Oh.'
He stands like a giant grasshopper which might fall over at any moment. He flirts with his pretty pink chequebook. It's almost part of him. I get mostly cash from him and a cheque to study the signature later.
  Afternoon Delight is on Capital. While he's elongating himself on me I focus my eyes on some random grey hairs on his body. 'Why wait until the cold midnight?' sings the radio. I think of people who can only have sex at night and clients having to take time off from something to have sex. I wonder why afternoons seem feminine and mornings masculine. And nighttime is bisexual or hermaphrodite.
  I look at more of his hairs. When I've finished my retreat, I'll go to an acupuncture clinic, something like that if I need to, not to orthodox healers. The client is bounding around me. Maybe he's old, but quite well preserved. Maybe I won't need acupuncture when I'm in the world again. He has a sour liquor smell and pulls his rubber off flamboyantly.
  'I'm Grey Flannel. I live at Foursome Square,' he says, 'number 444. That was really nice. I'll see your afternoons are soon kept for me. What are you doing at Christmas – going home?'

'Yes, that's right.' I cover myself. As I close the door after him, instead of smiling I laugh softly and wonder why.

It's Christmas Day and Boxing Day. The room is clean, tidied and prepared. My hair is washed. I'm showered, cleansed and manicured. I lie on soft nylon sheets and smell jasmine incense coming from the bathroom. A packet of Japanese seaweed soup is in the cupboard. On these precious days the silence is complete, both inside and outside. I let myself be touched by the softness of it, I feel it going through me. I've completed the first year on my own. I've never done anything this long. Foursome Square. I remember being there at 449 for three weeks as an au pair. A family of five who dressed up all the time and treated me according to the clothes I was wearing then: one pair of black trousers, split at the crotch, which split again when I mended them. Feeling weak all the time, wondering if I had enough strength to get through the time I would have to live. The tiny, claustrophobic, expensive houses there.

The world outside starts again and the phone is alive. The day is mild and rainy. I light patchouli incense and look through a magazine. There's a story about a prostitute. It starts out that she's young and pretty and happy and has sex with men because she likes it, and then gradually it becomes impersonal. She becomes older, not pretty, unhappy, and goes downhill. That's all there is to the story. There's no difference between social and work sex. It's a modern magazine for girls. The story sounds really Victorian.

A client comes in grinning under his raindrops. I hand him a rainbow-striped towel and he wipes them away.

'I'm quite together about this, you know,' he says. 'I can get a fuck. I just want a gentle massage. I work in a home for adolescent boys who have personality problems. Every now and then I have to attend a case meeting in Hampstead. You know what that is? It's a meeting with social workers and so on. This is the sort of antidote I need.'

I study him massaging my body. His fingertips aren't bad. The phone purrs . . .

'Hello . . . Hello . . . Hello . . . How are you?'

'Fine, thank you.'

'You know who it is, don't you?'

'I think so,' before I can remember. I nod, smile and wave to the social worker so he can leave. Grey Flannel has more to say than the average caller. When the buzzer goes, I say, 'Bye-bye.'

The next client is sharp-faced and darkly dressed. He stands in the corner.

'Now I must point out first of all that I'm allergic to rubber. I can't use rubbers.'

'Well, I'm allergic to not using them.' I move towards the door. 'Sorry.'

'Now, I insist. It would be a terrible thing for me. I work in the tax office.' He gets sharper and tenser. 'We've been trying to get someone in this house. If you lie, you'll go to prison.'

I open and shut the door on him. 'You'll go to prison!'

'You look after your teeth well.' At the dentist's I'm called Clover Star again. He's quite a posh dentist. My legs are higher than my head and there's music. I shut my eyes and feel his breath of clean nicotine as he examines my mouth. I watch him working, as he's trained to, and using his instruments. Mouths must get boring to work in after a while. I prefer cocks to work on.

At the special clinic at Shimmering Hospital under the soft ceiling lights the speculum emerges. I think, as I'm declared clean again, about the infections I had before. Then I think, now I've got used to metal inside me, I could have a coil easily and then my body would be free of drugs completely. I see the auxiliary has the shakes from doctor-given drugs.

'You're one of the family now,' says the nurse. 'See you soon.'

I smile. As I go down the corridor I remember Grey Flannel said he worked here. I hope he doesn't see me. It might worry him.

I send off for a back number of *Spare Rib* with an article on the coil, to prepare myself with facts before asking for what I want.

At the pill clinic the nurse takes my blood pressure, which I enjoy. But she hides the numbers from me and for five minutes I try to get her to tell me what it is. The doctor tells me, as if it's a big thing, that I've lost three pounds since last time.

'Yeah, well, I go up a stone or two and down a stone or two quite often,' I say. 'Not as much as I used to, though.'

'You mean a pound or two, surely.'

'No, I mean a stone or two.'

He doesn't believe me. I tell him I want the coil and what I know about it and why I want it.

'You know what your periods are?' he asks.

'Yes, they're like being cleansed out.'

'No, they're not.' Then he tells me in different words what comes to the same thing.

At the coil clinic, I come in while the squarish lady

doctor is finishing telling her assistant a joke. I try to guess the beginning. As I lie on the table they go through a new lot of coils on the shelf.

'Hey, this looks a nasty one. I wouldn't like to have to fit this one. What do you think?' As I lie, objectlike, on the table.

'We're just measuring you,' she says, 'so we get you one of the right size.' And she inserts something.

'What size am I?'

'B.'

'How many sizes are there?'

'A, B and C.'

I think of wombs coming in three standard sizes and giggle to myself.

'Can I see it before it's inserted?'

'Oh, all right, just a quick peep.'

It's S-shaped in sexy white plastic. It's called Lipps Loop, which seems to suggest World War I flying aces. As they put it in, I enjoy a little contraction.

'Would you like a cup of coffee or tea?'

'Coffee, please,' I say, before I remember that I don't drink coffee now. It has a wickedly alien taste and I feel as if it has put something different into my brain, but when I get outside it clears.

In Peachy Hill, a girl is sitting on a low wall crying.

'What's the matter?'

She's just got her Social Security money, started to do some shopping and lost the rest of it. She smells of cider and lives round the corner. I go up to her room with her. It's higgledy-piggledy. She's called Carmel and her boyfriend knocks her about, they row and she has no job. I give her the money I have on me and accept tea with dried milk, an unfamiliar colour and taste.

'Where do you live?' she says.

'Oh, round the corner,' to protect myself.

The darkly dressed client appears. This time he uses a rubber. I get my clothes on before he does and, as he's dressing, I sip some peppermint tea.

'What's that?'

'Herb tea.'

'You a vegetarian, then?'

'Yes.'

'I used to be. I'm a black magician and when you get to a certain stage of power you can eat meat, smoke, anything,' he says, lighting a fag and looking at my fairground tiger.

'We have periods of fasting when necessary.'

'Yes, I fast too, it's good.'

'We fast before a ceremony, then we have a sacrifice, an ox or goat, and we have to finish it up.'

I imagine trying to stomach that.

'Are you interested in magic?'

'Yes.'

I remember Moralag, a Mauritian musician who had sex with succubi, and sucking him off in the lift of the Civil Service Club. He wanted me to become his high priestess but I decided not to at the last minute. He told me his balls came off seven times and seven is a lucky number.

'Well, perhaps we can get together and I'll tell you more about it.'

'Yes, perhaps.'

He leaves peacefully without talking of prison or income tax.

At Oxford Circus, among the crowds, I get a glimpse of a girl wearing a black velvet cloak with a sequin pattern around the shoulders. I try to look at it again but lose her. When I find the right cloak in Kensington Market I buy sequins to decorate it. The lining is a gold-silvery lamé. I smile in shops when I buy things and ask them not to give me paper bags, to save trees.

In Baker Street a young guy with bare feet wants some money for lunch.

'Do you need some shoes as well?'

'No.'

I give him what I have.

I eat honey 'from the wild Tasmanian Leatherwood tree'. It's the least sweet and subtle honey I've tasted. I can smell the difference in each honey I get.

On telly Dave Allen is interviewing a man who lives as a recluse somewhere in the mountains of Oregon. I admire the guy. He has only what he needs, living off the land. In London, the land has been hammered and crushed, flattened by people and buildings and civiliza-tion. Once it was a marsh. I think I have the best of both, the advantages of solitude yet the feeling I'm doing my duty by being with people, the advantages of sex, the pleasures of celibacy. I know people, I know myself.

Clients who call themselves regulars sometimes want to come at the same time each week, but I avoid putting any such pattern into my life.

'I'm doing business with lots of Arabs, could put some really good business your way. They'll pay more than this. You help me, I'll help you.'

And I avoid letting them control the work like that.

'A party of us, it's a big business deal. It'd really help. Money's no object.'

I don't want to be involved in business deals, I don't like business. So I decline.

'You can't have any respect for yourself, doing this sort of thing,' says a client, pulling off his rubber.

'Why?' I offer him some tissues.

'Well, I mean, you can't, can you? It can't be good for you.'

'Oh.' I brush my hair.

I distil the remarks, brush them out of my hair and wash my hands of them. I put herb-smelling lotion on my hands.

I stroke my hands down a client's spine. When he turns over I enclose his cock with a rubber and stroke him, while I observe moles, freckles, bumps of muscles and face. He talks. I look at his breathing and his mouth and his rubbered cock and naked balls. He talks about money, the story of his Barclaycard, bank accounts, income tax, business, where to put one's money, what to do with it. I open my ears to these new things while I wank him. How can he talk about money while he's being wanked? I wonder. Anyway, some of it might be useful to me. I remember reading somewhere that the Victorian slang for ejaculation was 'spend'. I imagine little Barclaycards spurting out of him.

At Blodminster the landlady is on holiday. I stay with her neighbour. She's in her thirties and has a daughter of fourteen. I share a room with the daughter and look at the David Bowie pictures. In the evening when I've put Bill on the bus at the right time, the mother says, 'I envy you in a way. You can do what I've never been able to do with my daughter. You can give your kids your whole attention. Each time you see them, you devote it to them. With me there's always something else I have to do as well.'

As I leave the library, I glance at the beautiful, heavy,

imprisoned hair of the woman behind the desk. I reach into my pocket for bus money. I've left my purse in the loo at the library. I go back, but it's not there. I remember a woman who came in as I went out. It must have been her. I walk home, annoyed. Realize how near I am to Foursome Square. The day I got the sack from Foursome Square I had nowhere to go. And that was the day I had all my money – four weeks' wages – pinched. Funny, it's the same amount as was in that purse, £40, but I don't need it now. I hope it will do something for the woman. Perhaps she needs an abortion. It would just cover that.

'Cheer up, love, it may never happen!'

The horoscope says it'll be a good week for manual work. Well, I'll have a period, so that's likely. An article in *Spare Rib* about sexual harassment at work. A woman has been sacked because she rejected her boss's advances.

Grey Flannel rings up and chats on and on with lots of information. It's a novelty listening to him talking about this and that on the phone, about something other than my tits. He has lots of free afternoons.

'I'm surrounded by my bits of paper,' he says.

He has many afternoon appointments and pays afterwards, doing a flirtatious dance with his chequebook, which he refers to coyly. He lies on the bed and chats to me. I give him a sip of peppermint tea. He has a very straight marriage so can only see me in the afternoon. That's good. My retreat can be preserved. He fits into work and nothing can be taken from my private life. My eyes take in little sprouting hairs on his chin.

12

Mothers and Gingerbread Ladies

'I want to please you.'

'Is that OK?'

'Tell me if I do anything you don't like.'

I smile inside and let them in the door and out of the door, lock it again with the silver key. In the grey afternoon I lie on the bed in a soft pool of light from the cherub lamp and read about the 'troops out' movement, and the *TV Times* horoscope. I hear the voices from the phone-in programmes. I listen more and understand more.

I get minicabs to go into the centre of London in the middle of the afternoon when I feel the need to be clothed and moving about. Coming back on bright red buses, I watch middle-aged and elderly women in middle-aged or elderly uniforms smiling apologetically at their own slowness as they are jolted and jostled by the bus. And, as each one gets on, they create a community of sympathy for the jolted one. I worked in a hospital for three weeks just after I left school. That's where I met Olive. She had newly become a granny and, according to her clothing, was 'old'. One day I was looking at her arm and I saw that her arm wasn't old. Her arm told me that we were closer than I thought, and I started to see how we all become separated from each other.

At Peachy Rise, there are three tenants together in the hall. They look threatening. I walk in, not showing them anything. In the room, I free myself of them, but something is happening and I wonder what.

I wash the outside grit off my face and answer the phone. My body is getting more controlled, more capable as I learn to slide and adapt to avoid clients' clumsiness. Through the lacy curtains I watch neighbouring rooftops bobbing up and down with my chin on a gleaming shoulder. I am changing my past, whirling it around, refreshed and renewed. Like my washing every Thursday, turning and whirling in the launderette, all their smells and moisture washed from my clothes and fabrics. Even my future looks cleaner. To clients I am in their present. They attach the act, and me with it, by various threads to their 'real life' in the 'real world'.

'You do it for the money then?'
'Got a baby?'
'Where do you live?'
'Where do you go to enjoy yourself?'
'What do you do with your boyfriend?'

And I let the questions melt away. For me the event doesn't touch my private life, but I can look at it from my private self. They leave their clothes on the black silk cushions, and I leave mine as separately as possible. My body's weight doesn't change much now. Soon I can become just one person in every sense, feeling every step of the ground I walk on. I watch them examining my anatomy as if they've never seen a body before. An Irish guy in priestly black. He says he's a virgin. The second he comes the doorbell rings. Perhaps bells will always ring for him.

It's a windy February and grit blows about outside. They have coughs and colds and talk about what to take for them. I breathe all their germs, but I never catch anything. I listen to my voice on the phone and feel it in my body. And I hear more texture to the voices over the phone. Cocks curve and move all over the place. I avoid their eyes, and the dirt on their hands never stays in the room.

'Wank me.'

'Suck me.'

'Fuck me.'

In the park I see white, moist snowdrops rising from the grey land. Will I be ready in time for the spring?

Pyrrhus is in the hall.

'Could I have a word with you?'

I let him into the room. I don't lock the door as I would with clients. He's the only person apart from the handyman from *Time Out* to come into the room.

'Some people here have been complaining, saying you're running a brothel, and a red Cortina has been watching the place. Have you seen one?'

'No.'

'Well, best to cool it for a few days. It'll be OK then.'

The phone rings but I don't answer it in front of Pyrrhus. Later, on the phone:

'Do you visit?'

'Well . . . yes.' I'll see what happens.

I take a minicab to 29 Piebald Avenue in the Green Belt. I feel the chamois leather of my new coat against my tights. The movement of the machine is a treat for me. I pay the driver. I hide the rubbers in my purse.

Number 29 is the only one left in the avenue. All the others have been demolished. Sam is in bed when I get there. He has leather Eastern slippers and smells of being in bed with a cold.

The room is high-ceilinged with clowns on the walls. I like the room but it feels different from mine. Not

quite correct to do it here, I think as I stroke him.
Afterwards we sit in upright chairs. He offers me tea,
coffee, brandy. I have fruit juice and he has coffee. He
stays in this room when he's in England. The woman
who owns the house will never let it be knocked down.
I look through the large window into the garden at the
back. It seems to lead down to a river. I look at the
massive clowns' faces on the walls.

'The son painted them,' Sam says. 'There is one too
sad to be seen so I covered it with that wardrobe.'

Sam is going to Shimmering Hospital tomorrow to
have catheters put through his arteries to test his heart.
He might die. He has accepted that. Or they might
improve his condition. He tells me the story of going to
specialists in Sweden and other places, and I look at the
beautiful clowns and at his eyes, which seem to be
made to see across deserts. I ask him what he does. He
travels a lot because he deals in antiques. It seems a pity
to be a businessman. If he survives he will breed horses.
I like that. He invites me to come and ride them and I
accept it in a token way. When I leave, I tell him I'll
catch a cab, which is what he'd expect me to do. Instead
I walk around and get a bus. I conceal the extra rubber
as I pay my fare.

Grey Flannel phones the next day. He talks on and
on about his bits of paper and names he has forgotten.

Pyrrhus says it's OK again so the next day is full of
entwining in front of the mirror and birds start to sing
English bird songs outside. On the radio a woman is
talking about Gingerbread – single parents' self-help
groups. I take down the London phone number.
Instead of paying a landlord in Blodminster, maybe I
could baby-sit for someone in exchange for a bed, then
we'd both benefit.

So I meet Amanda Fudge and her son Joe, who's a bit younger than mine. She and her friend Gillian are younger than me but they seem much older. They drink coffee and smoke long cigarettes and speak on the phone to people about what they've said to other people. Amanda has beautiful skin on her face but she doesn't wash it much. Gillian has three kids. They talk about their children as if they were from another race.

'D'you want to go up the hill with the kids? Or come in for a cup of coffee?' I go up the hill with the kids.

In the evening Amanda puts on a record. She brings out lots of clothes, smelling of scent.

'I don't know what to wear yet. Do you like Neil Diamond?'

'Mmm, yeah,' I say out of habit. That must be him being played, I suppose. 'Well, I like music,' I say, 'but I can't recognize any of it. I mean, when I lived in Tottenham, I knew it was reggae 'cos all the parties and guys I knew were black and played it. I enjoyed it but I couldn't recognize it or be sure it was reggae if I heard it somewhere else. Once I thought I heard them say on the radio they were going to play reggae, so it sounded like reggae, but afterwards the DJ said it was the Beach Boys.' It's good to confess.

She has warm large brown eyes and blonde hair. I choose a tan, silky dress for her to wear.

Joe is in bed and I'm by myself. The flat is strewn with lots of things. The kitchen has kitcheny posters in it. The idea of a kitchen seems an ugly one. I don't need one. My present life revolves simply around my bed. The kitchen has lots of half-used, smelly sauces in jars, yet she doesn't like cookery.

On the telly there's a programme about a singer called Bette Midler. She stands under a simple spotlight and, holding a microphone, wows a whole audience. If I could sing, it would be nice to do that. Then they show what is behind the singer: managers, agents, photographers, people to tell her where to go, what to sing, what to wear. In the last scene someone is painting Bette Midler's toenails. Even her toenails aren't her own. I look at my naked feet. I certainly have the best deal.

Next time I go to Blodminster, I sit with the grownups. I've had a Friday without working and have spent the morning peacefully, cleaning the room, washing and cleaning myself. The excitement of travelling to Blodminster and being anonymous, clothed in weekend clothes and watching other clothed people and feeling fresh inside. Little black and beige lambs in the fields on the way up. Two guys opposite me. One is an anaesthetist and the other a private consultant. I hear them referring to patients as 'cannon fodder'. One offers to help me with my bag. I decline his help.

Mandy hasn't been by herself at all. She has served school dinners, has been with Joe, has been on the phone. But she isn't satisfied. She needs to be with more people and needs the phone to ring more. Then she gets the call she wants. It's Hector Vector who'll be round to take her to a party. She doesn't wash, but keeps searching through her clothes to find what to wear. I talk to Joe and look at her clothes.

Hector Vector appears with Gillian. I feel the plushness of the carpet with my fingers, finish a card game with Joe and watch Hector Vector. He's sort of mousecoloured and avuncular. I couldn't imagine him having sex with anyone. The three of them are working very hard at smiling and laughing. 'What do you do?' 'What do you do in London?' 'Where do you go?' I smile back. 'Oh, lots of things.'

Next day I go with Bill and Ben to the fairground. We whirl around on the dodgems and the wind is on our faces. I sit with Amanda. The colour telly is on very loudly with lots of unrealistic red and green. She talks of Hector. She doesn't really like him.

'Let's face it, I've got to have someone to get me from place to place. At least I can get lifts from him. Otherwise I'd never get out and enjoy myself. He's all right on the whole, I suppose.' Then she criticizes him again while I watch the colours on the telly. She has to have friendships to get transport.

'You must feel awful not being with your kids,' says Gillian.

'No, I don't. It's what I want.' I try not to feel guilty about it. It's the first time I've dared to tell the truth about that. The first time people have seen me as a mother. When I was with my children before, no one would believe I was their mother, not even me. These people let me have the right not to want what they want. Their ex-husbands surround their lives. Amanda and Gillian can't get rid of them. They are caught, dependent on their money, and the money is dependent on telling lies.

Going home on the train, it's dark, so I can't see the lambs in the fields. I look forward to being in the room again with my copy of *Spare Rib*. An article about a woman who 'got out of prostitution'. I save it till I get back, and just enjoy watching bodies in clothes and the lights in the train, and the feeling of moving to where I want to be.

The room is still there, softly glowing. Nicotine smell on my hair. I light sandalwood incense, shower and refresh myself. Into my blue cocoon of nylon and I look at the cherubs on the lamp.

The woman in the article 'had to' make herself available to clients twenty-four hours a day. They called when they felt like it. She went out with them and had to pretend to agree with them. She had to drink and smoke and buy drink and cigarettes, colour TV and stereo and other ugly things; and her daughter lived with her and clients sometimes saw her daughter, so they saw her private life. She was on display all the time, like Amanda. She didn't seem to know how not to be. On display, available, like the woman at the ugly library desk with the electronic instrument and her beautiful bound hair.

Some time next day I start to emerge from my cocoon.

13
Climax

Grey Flannel takes to lying on the bed longer and longer afterward as well as chatting on the phone.

'It's just not a bloke and a prostitute, is it?' he says. On Capital there's a little song about love and April playing, and 'No' comes out of my mouth. He and the radio say more or less the same thing in the corner of my ear. And it's OK because he only comes during *Afternoon Delight* so it can't break my retreat, I think.

I buy an oyster-silver quilt and a red carpet and spray the television silver. I paint my walls, the first time I've ever decorated anywhere. No possibility of decorating in my life before. The nearest thing was when a guy on the run from a circus painted a room we stayed in a while.

A hunched-up client comes through the door. He wants to come for less.

'Then I'll be round here regularly, twice a week,' he says, as if I need him.

'No.' I open the door wide. I don't need anyone particular as a client. I'm free of them. I sit in a minicab when I suddenly want to be away and by myself.

Grey Flannel brings a poster out of his briefcase. It's of women around a car. CUSTOM CAR, it says. When he's gone I look at it. It's some car or other with five women draped round it in positions of subservience. I put it away in the cupboard.

'Grey,' I say, testing the feel of a personal name.

'I love the way you say that.'

Although he drives a car, his fingers feel as if they touch people. I see in his hands there is more there than he has developed.

'It's funny,' he tells me, 'my sister-in-law had bronchitis. I examined her chest with a stethoscope. She got all coy afterwards because I'd seen her breasts.'

Later, I elude a heavy car driver twisting my nipple as if it's an ignition key, and distract him into doing something else.

'And the Hammersmith bypass is chock-a-block,' says Capital.

When he's gone I flick to David Simmons. It's the Friday problem time. He takes time and really listens to people. There are silences while he thinks about their problems or gives them time to say something. The silences are alive, the best radio ever.

'Dawn,' says Grey Flannel. I may never be Clover again. What will I be called in my future private life? I lift up the oyster quilt for him.

Grey phones me from Shimmering Hospital.

'Dawn, Dawn, Dawn. I don't give a fuck if all this goes through the switchboard and everyone hears.'

'I think you get through patients quicker than I get through clients.'

'What are they?' says a client looking at my tits.

'Pardon?'

'What do they measure?'

I cover my amazement and throw out some measurements to satisfy his need for numbers. If they can see, why do they need measurements?

'I'm nineteen, is that all right?'

'I'm fifty-nine, is that all right?'

'I'm seventy-five, is that all right?'

'I'm forty-four.'

'I'm thirty-five.'

'I'm twenty-five.'

'Oh.' Does that matter here, now?

'How long for?'

'How long will it take?'

'How much time can I have?'

I produce some segments of time for them.

A client who's been before. He's in the rag trade.

'It's really because my wife's pregnant,' he says. 'She's quite short, you know, and it's pressing against her ribcage very uncomfortably.'

I don't feel the pain immediately, but my ribs feel distorted off and on for a few days afterwards. I try to stop it by telling myself that, after the birth, the pains will have gone.

A client in a pinstripe suit with a soft face. In a confidential way he says, 'Will you do this for me? This is what I'd like. I want a needle put into my balls. I used to go to a girl who did it, but she's not around any more.'

Can I bear his pain? I wonder, but he'll enjoy it, so it won't hurt. Do I need to feel other people's physical pain?

We discuss the price of a needle in his balls. I open the cupboard discreetly, so he can see none of my private things, and get a darning needle. I prick it into his slug-coloured balls a few times and there is no pain. But he wants me to stick it in once and wiggle it a bit. When he's gone there's a new feeling, that I may not need to feel people's pain. I brush my hair, following the line of the mantelpiece which looks too heavy and wintery for the sun outside.

* * *

I phone a visiting hairdresser in *Time Out* and get to meet Allsop. He's pink and clean with nice-coloured clothes. He enjoys the herb tea I make him.

'You've got a nice voice,' he says as he trims my hair.

'I used to do acting. I'm doing massage, now.'

We chat over herb tea and nuts. He tells me of the person who shared his flat and who split, hurting him. As he says 'person', I think he must be gay but not quite able to say so.

The phone rings. I prepare to hear Grey Flannel.

'Hello, this is your friendly neighbourhood black magician.'

'Oh.'

'You sound disappointed. Don't you want to be in on a sacrifice?'

'Well, some other time perhaps.'

Grey Flannel is walking round the room. He produces his chequebook with practised, stylized hand movements. He flirts with a pretty pink virginal cheque and finally impregnates it with his pen.

At Blodminster, I'm still called Clover. In the sun I roll down a hill with the kids and sting my hand on baby nettles.

Next week the pinstripe-suited client appears and talks about having bits of his balls cut with a razor. We discuss it for a while and he says he'll come back with a suitable razor.

Grey Flannel is on the phone and I'm looking through the *Leveller*.

'Why do you go up to Blodminster?'

'My kids are up there.'

'Oh, what a faithful mother.' He goes on. I feel his sadness coming through the telephone, and then tears coming down my cheeks.

'I'm crying,' I say.

'So'm I,' he says.

I'd forgotten that there was crying. It seems to break the peace.

I put an ad in *Time Out* to get a lift to Blodminster instead of the train. To share a car and petrol seems a good idea. A guy, with a *café au lait* car, which bounces, answers nicely. Grey Flannel tells me it is the make of car that managing directors often have. He chuckles and smiles. I don't understand why. Then it hits me. He thinks I have sex with the guy in exchange for lifts. That would be impossible.

'I'm not a prostitute when I'm not working. I just work as one.'

'But you are,' he says. He doesn't have a clue.

'I'm not one twenty-four hours a day.'

Outside there is more sun and several backs of heads look like Grey's.

Next time, as he's stroking his pink cheques: 'If it's like this you shouldn't have to pay me. But because you see me during working time in the afternoons, I think you should compensate me for the money I would make. Do you think that's right?'

'Yes, that's all right.'

I alight on a sum. I halve it and give it attractive digits and he says he'll let me have it soon. I'm glad to be finished with that. Next time I wear new jeans.

'Not your working clothes?' He seems to understand what it means.

I'm glad to be free of his cheques.

At the local law centre, I want to find out if I have any chance of getting my kids to stay overnight at Amanda's so I can see more of them. I wear jeans, hair pulled back, my hands feel nervous. I see a guy of about thirty who'd look quite nice cleaned up. As with clients, I feel he's an equal. Before, I would have discounted him because he's fair and freckled and I don't find him sexy. His back is rounded and his chest a bit hollow, not from being a car driver, I think, but just from hunching his shoulders. I consider his fair, hairy hands with smoke coming up between the fingers.

'I was put in a mental hospital illegally for a couple of months. How will that count against me?'

'Well, we've all been in mental hospitals, haven't we?' he says, hunching more.

'And I've, er, been working in a massage parlour,' I venture, trying the water.

'No problem, no problem. I think you should get Flora Fedora. She's got a beautiful office, really casual, you sit on floor cushions, and she's really into women's rights.'

'Oh. OK, thanks.'

I take down the solicitor's name and number.

Grey says, 'Come on, let's go for a drink at the pub by Shimmering Hospital.'

Walking along Peachy Rise with someone is strange. He hovers before and after me as we walk. He opens the door to the minicab office, and I and the manager smile in the usual relaxed way. I enter the office, then feel a sudden change. The manager and the driver focus on Grey and almost draw themselves to attention. The yellow-wigged driver with whom I usually sit in the front opens the door for us and we are in the back. He acts as if I'm not there, or rather, I feel I've become something else. He is full of cap-doffing movements though he hasn't got a cap.

We draw up outside the Fertile Frog. The sun shines outside. We penetrate the inside which is gloomy,

smoky and full of people making noise. There is a
sweetened fruit juice in front of me. Grey's hands are
shaking as he downs a drink without pleasure. The two
other people at the table have plates of food in front of
them and massive glasses of beer. The guy has a mental-
hospital or prison-officer look. His plate is full of dark-
brown stewed mince and mashed potato. The woman
has almost completely uncovered and exposed the grey
bones of her chicken. Smoke is advancing on it from
Grey's shaking fingers. She is talking about a patient.
'She's really strange, vegetarian, you know.' She swal-
lows a mound of grey-white mashed potato and lights
a cigarette.

Later, I tell Grey I'm going to see Flora Fedora.

'Why don't you go to my solicitor? He's really good. I
can mention you to him. That's the best idea,' he says
on the phone.

'No, it's all right, thanks. First I'll try her.'

It seems a good idea that a woman should be my
solicitor. And if I have a solicitor, it should be mine and
not his.

'Let's go to Lords. Have you ever been? I'm a
member, you know. It's such a silly game, cricket. I
love it.'

It's an amazing, hot April day. I have an appointment
with Flora Fedora, then I'm going to meet Grey at the
Lord's Tavern.

In her office my jeans feel tight as I sink into a saggy,
beige, corduroy cushion-chair. The room has lots of
abstract man-made tits in it, many in Perspex. Her
nipples are covered with a black cotton T-shirt. Her hair
matches it, and she's wearing turquoise espadrilles with
ties round the ankles. She asks questions about times
and dates and ages. It seems a good idea, if you have to

have a solicitor, to have one nice to look at. I'd better get it over with. Soon I'll be out of here and in the sun, but I have to ask the question first.

'I do massage. I work as a prostitute. Does that make any difference?'

She's about forty but I feel on an equal level with her. I'd have been frightened of speaking to anyone of that age before.

'Yes, it would be really counted against you. It's ironic. The judge probably goes somewhere himself for a "French massage".' She moves her fingers as if playing the piano on someone's back. 'Yet he will condemn you out of hand for doing what is done to him. Yes, I would very much like to fight this case as a matter of principle. But I must tell you your chances of winning are not very high. Perhaps you'd like to think about it.'

'Yes, thank you.'

On the steps of the Lord's Tavern, Grey is sitting dappled with sunlight. My tomato juice is standing next to him and the ice has completely melted. I have to admit I like where I am. I feel settled.

'It's eighty degrees, they said on the radio. Isn't it marvellous?'

We watch the white, bright cotton moving in the sun, and I feel the wooden bench against my clothes.

'I'm starting a novel about us,' says Grey. 'Read the beginning.' He gives me some black pen-covered sheets of white paper.

I read. 'I first met Dawn on a newsagent's board in northwest London,' it begins.

'But if you write about it, it's not real any more,' I say. And remember having to sit dumbly receiving poems about me, trying to stop myself giggling in case it hurt someone personally and feeling that the poem was more about the person who wrote it than about me.

'Are you an alcoholic?' I ask him.

'No, I'm not. You wouldn't want to have anything to do with me if I was, would you?'

'I just wanted to know, that's all.'

I feel the sunshine.

'I've got a nice solicitor who doesn't wear a bra,' I say.

'I've started eight novels,' says Grey, and we watch the cricket.

Grey's wife is being sterilized in Harley Street. I don't know very much about the operation; I try not to think of it. My period goes on for eleven days and gives me different feelings from usual.

'Did she have much pain and did she bleed?' I ask Grey the day after it stops.

'There was slight discomfort and the bleeding stopped yesterday. She's all right now.' There should be an end to other pain; I don't have to suffer it.

In the garden behind Peachy Rise I put my oiled arm over my face and see fluttery rainbow rings where my skin touches the sky, and the English sun becomes real. I do self-hypnosis and find my beach is here, too. I want to be here. But I'm not going as deep with hypnosis as I used to. I come out of it, turn on my stomach and my oiled fingers mark *Time Out*. 'Hypnotist. Consultation by appointment. Blair Bell.' By myself in my cool room, I do a headstand for the first time.

On the phone the hypnotist has a nice American accent, like Bondini who first taught me.

Then Grey rings up. I ask about his wife. 'A very good gynaecologist. You should go if you need one,' he says. 'I'll put you on to him. I've used him before. He did an abortion for me.' He laughs comfortably. 'Do you want me to mention you?'

'No, thanks.'

I don't want to go to Harley Street. It sounds like he's putting me on a plate for the gynaecologist.

'Let's go away for a couple of days somewhere. I've just bought a little car. Anywhere.'

'Frillingford. My kids support that football team. It's in Surrey.'

'Never heard of it. I'm sure it doesn't exist, that team.'

'Oh yes, they've got rainbow-striped scarves and they've just opened a club shop, so I can get all the gear for the kids. They can never get them. Blodminster is too far away.'

'End of next week we'll go to this unbelievable place of yours, then.'

The Tuesday before that I have a midafternoon appointment with Blair Bell, hypnotist. I lie on an old-fashioned grey velvet-covered couch. There are purple velvet curtains, drawn. It's a basement room, hidden from the sun and lit by candles and a lamp.

He goes through the colours of the prism as Bondini did. I take over and my feet start melting and the rest of my body melts so I hardly feel the couch. When I get up, I know what I must ask him and tell him.

He has a black velvet smoking jacket, glossy black hair and lazy, smiling eyes.

'I want to stop feeling other people's physical pain,' I say. 'I've always felt it, as long as I can remember. At first I just accepted it 'cos I thought everyone was like that.'

'I suggest you use a unique, happy scene to protect you from it, to help you realize you don't need to feel others' pain.'

I choose swimming and splashing in blue water.

'You know you can change this from something negative to something positive. This feeling of pain might be transformed into healing people. You may have a gift for healing.'

Back in the room I lie on my tummy on a smooth sheet, and a rubbered cock goes between my thighs while I think about healing and splashing in the water.

Next day I fast and practise self-hypnosis with the new scene, stand on my head a bit and phone Grey. He's going to pick me up the next day to go to Frillingford.

The sky is blue with soft clouds. I listen to the words of songs on the radio and feel the vibration of the car.

'There's a health-food shop,' I say.

'There's a hospital,' Grey said. 'Why do you notice health-food shops and I notice hospitals?'

Grey handles parts of his car the way he touches his chequebook, and at the hotel desk he looks at ease. We walk through some narrow streets with lots of yellow lines on them. I go into the shops and buy rainbow-striped scarves and rosettes.

Over Chinese food, I say, 'I've been having a sort of retreat and, when I come out of it, I'll give myself a new name.'

We carry the rainbow items to the hotel room. I look at myself in the mirror. I'm in a cream jacket I've never worn. I've saved it for some time. I think Melissa is the name I'll choose.

And now on the bed I cover every atom of him, and as he touches me I feel every atom of me, and I feel and he touches me in all the places clients don't. Everything sharper, stronger, so much more than before. I've come here from a two-year sex time capsule. In the past, sex was a misty, soft blur and so was I. Before I worked as a prostitute, I just drifted. Now I focus on the whole body and enter part of me I've never entered before. I feel the part of his spine which has always given him trouble. I kneel over him and touch his spine gently and focus on it and concentrate on wishing to heal it. Later I stroke and rub him and he comes with a shock and a jerk. He's almost knocked sideways, subdued by it. I feel him diminishing.

'You really came then,' I say. Like never before, I think.

He says nothing.

During the night he trembles and sweats a lot. In the morning he's shaky, trembling and sweating.

'Are you all right?'

'Yes, I'll be OK.'

Later we sit on a grass verge, eating bread. Grey drinks some tomato juice and starts to be sick.

'I think we'd better go back to London now.' He is shaking more.

'What's wrong?'

'Nothing, but I think we'd better go back.'

At the hotel I pile all the rainbow-striped things in the car.

'There's only one and a half seat belts,' says Grey.

He puts one round me and drops the half one across his knee.

'It's symbolic somehow.'

We head for London up the motorway, his thigh shaking under the half seat belt, and listen to more words of songs. Up Foursome Road in the rush hour. 'My wife might be back now.'

Back at Peachy Rise, shaking, he picks up my phone to ring home. It's not working.

'You should lie down for a while. Something's wrong with you.'

'I must phone home. I'll use the call box in the road.' He goes out, and a few minutes later I go out and lean against his car and feel the sun and the blue sky and the hot bonnet.

Suddenly a scream from the phone box. I run in, hold him. He's convulsing, foaming at the mouth, jerking. The receiver is dangling from its cord. I put it back and phone 999, an ambulance. He hurls himself out of the box. I kneel and cushion his head on my thighs, wiping some foam from his chin. The convulsions pass through his body and gradually die out. His right hand remains rigid, clinging to a lock of my hair. And a stranger's reassuring voice says, 'Have you phoned an ambulance? Does he take any pills? Turn his head to one side. It's all right. The ambulance will be along in a moment. It always seems to take a long time. Do you know him?'

'No,' I say protectively. Grey is limp and breathing noisily. The guy tries to unclench his hand from my hair. 'Yes, well, I do know him.'

Then he lets Grey's hand be, as if it's all right for him to hold my hair since I know him.

The ambulance men help him to stand up.

'What's happened?' says Grey. 'Where's my jacket? I want my jacket.'

'Better go to Shimmering Hospital,' I say.

'You won't need it in hospital, mate,' they say.

I put the jacket on him because I know he needs it now. In Shimmering Casualty they look at me suspiciously. He's taken into a cubicle and forms are brought out. I can't pretend I don't know him. Hope they don't. It's a massive place. Give them his name and address.

'What's happening to him? Can I see him?'

'You'll have to wait.'

Walk up and down. If I smoked, I'd smoke now. I follow the corridor in the direction they're taking him. A woman in white, looking cold at a desk, tells me nothing. I get a glimpse of the cubicle where he's being examined. He's moving slowly and they are holding him. I feel he's falling apart. I lean against the wall, my legs too weak to hold me. What's happened to him could be my doing: he's pretty old. I'm scared, my legs get even weaker. I tell the doctor I want to speak to him. He tells me to wait, then comes out.

'What's he been doing today? What are his drinking habits?'

'I don't know. I don't know him well. Let me see him.'

In there Grey is trying to sit up.

'What's happened, what's happened?'

'It's all right, you're in hospital.'

'You must go, my wife'll be here soon. You must go before she sees you. She mustn't see you.'

'OK, I'll go. I'll be in touch. I'll phone the hospital.'

'Not tonight, she'll be here.'

There's nothing else I can do. At Peachy Rise my weakened legs are in contact with a client's. He's an all-in wrestler. Then I watch *Crossroads*.

14
The Pale Green Tree

It's Saturday the next day. I phone the hospital.

'Are you a relative?'

'No, a friend.'

'Well, we can't give you any details.'

I have to do something. I take my old bikini out of the cupboard – it has a bleached, salty, Pacific smell still – and go to the swimming baths.

'Er . . . were you in Aussie?'

Surfing blond hairs. I look at him. More questions.

'Yes.' I said hello to him a couple of times on the beach.

'You look really different now. Relaxed, outgoing, you're happy now, aren't you?'

'Yes.' I smile but don't try to bridge the gap between then and now. He gives me his phone number.

'See you some time.' I smile and enter the water. I think that if I fucked with him, it'd be the beach I'd really want to fuck, so it seems unnecessary to phone him. I float and turn to meet a vivid face. It's called Samantha. She wants to teach me to dive. It's something I've been scared of, but I must. We jump and splash first. In China there's a custom of putting a hot coin on someone's forehead to take a pain somewhere else. Diving becomes a hot coin. I must have fear to stop fearing for Grey.

Samantha and I sit in a new ice-cream parlour, all in white, licking peach ice cream. Outside the earth is cracking up in a heatwave. Samantha's eleven and tall for her age.

'I'm Clover,' I say.

'The hot dogs were lovely,' she says. 'Do you want to come to my mother's shop? It's Tasteful Artefacts in Peachy Road. She makes lace.'

I don't know about meeting people's parents. They're not always like the sons and daughters. Her face is eager for me to go with her.

'Yeah, OK.'

Henrietta Harp is talking about her epilepsy to a slow-moving guy. They are both epileptics. She's like a fine bird of prey with wild crowlike feet, wild hair and eyes. Her little, blue-white teeth are the sexiest part of her.

'My friend. He had a fit. Perhaps it was epilepsy. He foamed at the mouth.'

She tells me of her minor and major fits.

'What school do you go to?'

'I don't. I do massage.'

'I've got the kid and Orlando,' she says, pointing to a squirming baby on the floor. 'His father's just left us. I can't afford anything to make us a proper meal. We're going home to baked beans tonight.'

I give Samantha money to do some shopping. When she's gone, Henrietta says, 'I think she wants to go to your place to watch telly.'

'Well, I'd better warn you, I work as a prostitute. It's not a good idea,' I say, protecting myself.

She pushes Orlando's stroller and I skip along with Samantha. I get food for them in passing shops, tinned mangoes to taste for the first time. Her living room is full of artefacts from the shop. Now that Henrietta knows I'm nearer in age to her, she moves Samantha away from me and wants to talk to me alone. So I read a horse story to Samantha before she goes to bed and look forward to swimming with her soon.

'Lacemaking is what I really do. I sell other things in the shop, of course. You could help me with that and have a room here. You'd have to pay only half the rent and rates of this place. None of your lovers here. You can keep all your fruity lovers in your knocking shop.'

'They're not my lovers. Only Grey is. It's a job. It's a very nice job. I'm lucky, I think. The mother of a guy I knew in Sydney said I should get a factory job, something to leave my mind free to think. Well, I suppose my job could be called a glorified factory job. It's something I can do and yet be free, and all the conditions are mine. I can make the room what I like, wear what I like, work when I choose, speak when I choose. I don't have to think about what I'm doing unless I want to.'

Henrietta says, 'I've never fancied a man in my life. Samantha's father – it was love with him, but I never fancied him. The first time was with him, I got pregnant. We weren't married. He made me have an abortion. I've been hurt not once, but again and again. Orlando's father said to me, "Let's have a fuck." Can you imagine? If he'd provided us with a proper home, it would have been different. Then I'd have given him more loving sessions. He should have treated me as the mistress of the house. What I should have done is had my own home and a man to provide and treat me properly. I was using a cap but I lost it. That's how I got him, Orlando. I expect – what's he called – Grey will be round for his oats when he's out of hospital.'

How terrible to have sex clogged up with all this! I'm overwhelmed by pity for her. Imagine if I had heard someone talking like that before I'd ever had sex. I see how lucky I was to have had it undistorted by any words and surrounded by summer water. It was in a beautiful house, all white inside and out, on its own island. I was nine. A little river ran past the front and back doors and on either side was a little wooden bridge. Every window looked out on water. Smell of weeping willows on water. From the breakfast table we threw home-made bread to the swans and cygnets swimming past. He was an artist and film-set designer. It was the first time I was aware of choosing what I wanted. All the white walls and ceilings were covered with his paintings from the time he lived in a Moorish castle in Spain – people and places from there – and in every door panel gypsy scenes. Even the furniture was white, with his little flower designs painted on handles of drawers. One whole ceiling of cherubs flying in clouds. I liked him painting me, and I liked playing with the papier-mâché puppets he made. I looked at his paintings and saw a brownish sandy-mauve there. 'Why do you put mauve in every one?' 'Because mauve is the shadow of life.' It gave me enough happiness to send me through most of my life. Later, I found he was probably my father's real father, but no one seemed to believe that very much. I thought he'd be quite nice to have as a grandfather.

'I have high standards,' Henrietta says. 'Look at that, now.' She points to a picture of a delicately rounded woman in pretty colours. 'Now, that's vulgar. What I sell in the shop, the lace I make, they're not like that.'

'Since I've been working,' I say, 'I've become discriminating about having sex in my private life. Before I worked as a prostitute, I would just have sex. I'd never thought about it, never really thought if I wanted to or not. I didn't know about wanting things then. I can see now the possibility of sex being something precious in a personal way. Before, it was the only thing that kept me going in life. I have more respect for people, since working as a prostitute, and I respect myself for the first time.'

I absorb her blue eyes. First time ever a friend with blue eyes and a friend who is a woman. Grey has green eyes. And Henrietta's a friend I don't have sex with. I sit on a silky chair for hours, talking, with pots of tea. Just talking and no sex. I never did that before. My voice was too weak to be heard and said 'Pardon' most of the time.

Henrietta says, 'Such a cosy feeling when you're pregnant, isn't it? You don't think? It's as if the rest of the world didn't exist.'

'No, I didn't feel cosy at all. I feel cosy now. When I was pregnant with Ben – it was funny – I was being fucked with a banana and nearly fucked by a Labrador. Ben grew up crazy about bananas and Labradors. I never thought of that till I was locked up and then I had to think of something funny to keep me going.'

At three in the morning I walk home, feeling so upset that I eat chips on the way. Next day, Sunday, I can't fast or be at peace because of what might happen to Grey.

On Monday Grey rings.

'Is it to do with drinking?'

'Oh! Yes, er . . . well, possibly.'

He's in the alcoholics' ward.

'Can I come and visit you?'

'No. It might not be safe. It's too risky. I'll be out soon. I'll phone you.'

* * *

'You got a boyfriend?'
    'What does he do?'
    'He plays in a band.'
    'He's coloured?'
    'Yeah.'
As I listen to myself I wonder why the boyfriend becomes coloured. Of course, because Grey is white. The hospital pay phone has a particular sound and for two days I listen to the sound of all the pay boxes from which I'm phoned. I can't bear waiting any more. I lie in the sun and watch all the beautiful insects, swim with Samantha and we go to Tasteful Artefacts.

Henrietta tells me about her bills, which are pinned up on the wall in front of her. She looks at them a lot. I pay some of them. It must be terrible to be thinking of money so much. She has her till in front of her all day. But she looks as if she despises her customers.

'See, they're doing that on purpose.'
    'What?'
    'And you're doing just what they want.'
    'What am I doing?'
'Looking at them, of course, those two guys. They're standing outside there. They're not interested in what's in the window. They just want you to look at them. I hate them. All men are bastards.'
    'I must go now.'
'Wasting fucking time, eh? Huh huh.' Her eyes implore me to stay and because she's so unhappy, I daren't show my happiness. It's not fair to her.

The heatwave is building up. I stop liking London and start loving it. In the street a girl is carrying a black cat in her arms and letting it lick a white ice-cream cone. I lie in the grass in the garden watching all the insects, active as never before. Thriving ladybirds and jolly spiders crawl over me. Turn over and the oiled inside of my elbow looks like a little cunt. Then a little cunt appears and pees on my library book. I wipe it off and say hello to May, who's three, a neighbour's child. Still sun-fucked, I wander into the room for an appointment that may happen.

Two people. I remember someone asking if a couple was all right, but sometimes they ask to bring their wives or girlfriends only because they like talking about it. A couple's never happened. It's two guys – one's been before – nice blond hair and turquoise shirt. I can't think what to do. I've got too much sun in me to do anything. Sucking and fucking happen, but they don't seem to want to touch each other. I've still got the sun inside me.

Grey comes out of hospital. He says 'for the rest of my life' instead of 'all my life', as people I knew before did. Henrietta does, too. They're older.

'We'll be separating soon. You could move in with me then.'

I see his claustrophobic, expensive house, and try to fit my future into it. It's hard work. And Henrietta wants me to share her flat. She thinks it would be 'good for me'. I look at Grey's sprouting hairs, look at my ceiling and breathe. Looking round the room, I flash forward to myself looking at this as the most beautiful place of my life. When he leaves, it's a different feeling from clients leaving. When they leave, I feel right and complete.

In Blodminster I give everyone fresh mangoes from London. Bill and Ben's stepmother, I hear, chopped up the immoral fruit of my immoral earnings and served them with tinned cream. As I smear some mango over my face and eat the rest, Gillian says, 'My ex-husband was in the Navy and he said there were two types of prostitutes – those who enjoyed it and those who didn't. The ones who didn't were all right.'

I lick mango and wonder what 'it' is.

When Gillian's gone, Mandy tells me what Gillian needs is a prostitute. Then she spends a long time describing the bum of a solicitor she was with. I get very bored indeed. Finally she leaves me baby-sitting with the guy next door.

Next day while I'm waiting for Bill to turn up she says, 'What happened? What did you talk about?'

'Vegetables, he knows a bit about them.'

'Oh,' she says, disappointed.

I bedeck Bill with Frillingford scarves and rosettes.

Grey isn't going back to work at the hospital. He's convalescing.

'You could do osteopathy,' I say. New things could start for him. The sky is blue and he wears blue denim over his grey hairs when I show him Tasteful Artefacts.

'Oh, how nice to see breastfeeding.'

'He's been on the tit a long time,' says Henrietta. I hope they like each other.

Customers come in and out. Henrietta talks about her prices. She takes all the prices personally. They are touched with emotion. Bills are still hanging around. Piles of paper to do with money. Too many objects in the shop to see them clearly. Grey pays court to her prices. He tantalizes her with his chequebook. Like a bird doing a courting dance, he moves around the shop. They talk about his being a doctor and she produces symptoms; about his firm, shares, his money; her cheque accounts, her prices, which he calls money going out and money going in. She draws attention to two battered paying-in books. She was telling me a long story about them last time. His chequebook hovers.

At work I get rid of money thoughts in a few seconds as the notes disappear. If clients talk of it, I open the door wide so they can leave. I think of how I was before, when I felt twelve and talked mostly to kids, fucked mostly with adults. I wouldn't like to be involved in a cheque account. I expose my eyelids to the sun, open them to the sun, and then in the whitened shop I feed me and Orlando with an orange.

When Grey's gone, I give Henrietta an envelope with money for some of the bills. Henrietta says, 'Yeah, I should do what you do – send Samantha and Orlando to their fucking fathers and fuck men and get paid for it – might get some lovers that way, too, huh huh.'

I flinch from the anger and hate and start crying.

'It's not like that. They're not my lovers. I don't feel like that. I don't think men are bastards.'

But it's cruel to her if I say that.

The phone rings and she grasps at it as if she needs it.

'Anyway, it won't do you any good if you carry on like this.'

'Why?'

'You'll go downhill. If you go on dressing the way you're doing. Look at those silly shoes.'

My new shoes to celebrate sun and being warm. 'They feel nice.'

We walk up the hill with Orlando. She tosses her head and says, 'Humph! They must know what you are.'

'Who?'

'Those men, the way they look at you. Did you hear what they said?'

'No, I don't listen to people in the street.' How can she connect that with what I do?

'They were talking about your tits.'

'Oh. D'you want some mangoes?'

'No, I couldn't eat anything, I've got bellyache. I wish I'd known you before you were doing this.'

I can just see it. She would have thought me trash then because I was dumb, stupid. She would have despised my clothes, the guys I had sex with, my voice and my weakness. Becoming a prostitute has made me a person she likes.

At Peachy with Grey:

'I like having my blood pressure taken. It really feels nice when it's being squeezed, let go and squeezed that bit more.'

'Oh. I'll have to come round and do it for you. I'll charge you, though.' We laugh. 'How much do you make?'

'What?'

'How much money do you make in a week?'

'Oh.' I give last week's amount.

'You're mercenary.'

'Why?'

'Well, you must be.'

And in the room at work I slide on silk and my cunt is kissed in a friendly fashion. As I shut the door on each client, I feel the smile on my face as usual. But as Grey Flannel leaves I feel 'like a prostitute' and wonder why. Grey goes on about living together. This time he suggests my children as well. I tell him things I never have before.

'Does it affect you that I work as a prostitute?'

'Oh no.'

Both he and Henrietta say I should put a time limit on what I'm doing. They use the word 'prostitute' a lot.

'Let's go somewhere else,' I say. It gets hotter, too hot for clients to come in the afternoon, sometimes too hot to touch. We smile and sweat. The beautiful heat makes them wash properly at last. I spend time in the garden getting browner and watching the insects. And the parks of London become interesting. The flat opaque green gets a golden depth, turns gold, then desert brown as the earth starts to crack. I buy the tight, tight jeans of the moment. 'No, it's OK, I can zip it up myself, thanks,' to the assistant who pats the zip. I decorate myself with summer clothes that I really like. And I like Grey for not reacting any differently. Whatever I wear, he makes no comment. Grey comes round to spend an evening with me, and brings a bottle. I pick up a pink sequin from the floor – and lay it on his prick.

'What's that for?'

'Just decoration.'

Doctors sometimes know less than patients. I think of him in a warm and comfortable car when Jed, I and the others were freezing, and of fucking with Jed on a bench in the grounds of the mental hospital. Now Grey has two cars but he's not free.

'That's a sensible way to pee,' I say, 'sitting down. Do you always do that?'

'Yes, I always have done. It's comfortable. Where's your television gone?'

'I gave it to Henrietta. I don't want to watch telly any more.'

'I've got four television sets in my house. I can't stand the things.'

When he's gone, the room is filled with smoke. Next day I start coughing.

'I can bring you some pills.'

'No, thanks.'

I stand on my head and try to answer the phone. There's a little twinge in my shoulders. I let Grey massage it. His fingers don't feel as if they know what they're doing. The twinge spreads down my arm. He sucks a lemon and I take a spoonful of honey and we kiss. He tells me how he has haggled for a lamp. The price was £1.20 but he managed to get it for a pound, after a while.

In the swimming baths with Samantha my arm and leg suddenly seize up. I think I'm drowning. 'Help!' I grab the only black guy there, and then I don't think I'm drowning any more. I wonder why. On the bus a black conductor is unrolling a long, white prick of ticket from his machine. I remember a guy from before with a white prick under black pubic hair. He couldn't do anything, and at that time I happened to stroke a smooth black tomcat. His erect tail was lovely.

'Cheer up, love!'

'You should buy a nice flat,' says Grey. 'Then I can come and visit you there.'

'I thought about buying a boat. That would be nice.'

'No, you should get property.'

Flora Fedora says, 'If you have property, it will help the court case. If you have property they will consider you 'respectable'. It's ridiculous, of course, but that's the way they work.'

Grey and Henrietta escort me round Hampstead estate agents. They pretend to be my relatives. I pretend to be someone else. Estate agents loll in heatwave postures with vague erections crawling along their thighs. Henrietta berates them. 'It doesn't seem real,' I say. They take down details of who I am and Henrietta's address, which I use to protect my privacy.

Sitting in Henrietta's shop, I say, 'What's that funny bobbly thing on that ornament.'

'That's a prostitute's thing.'

'What do you mean?'

'Well, it's the sort of thing a prostitute would have, isn't it?'

It's horrible.

'Come back with me tonight.' Her sad eyes plead.

Over tea we sit on her beautiful silky chairs and she says, 'I'm past my peak. Now it's all downhill.'

'It's terrible to believe that. Life can get better and better all the time. My life is better than ever.'

'No, I reached my peak a few years ago,' and she demonstrates what she believes with her hand. 'That's what life is. It happens to us all. It'll happen to you.'

'If you believe it, it'll happen.'

After that her lace designs stop looking beautiful.

In *Cosmopolitan*, an article about the male menopause. It could be Grey. It describes it as a psychological thing – a fantasy of wanting to branch out and change, to renew one's life. But why should that be a fantasy, denigrated by a stale medical term? Grey is like a husband from a TV play sometimes, but it's no good trying to fit people into theories. One should have faith in people – in what they can do.

In the garden I start to write to Grey:

What I am achieving by my present life situation is . . . a state of being so that, whatever happens to me, my personality can't be imprisoned in any way, so I can still be me. This is vital to me. It's my chance. I'm doing it. I can't set any time limit. It is slow because I know it's the right thing. To achieve this peace I made sure no one knew who I was. I made sure I got a rest from people, so I could become myself.

Having fasted for a day, I drink sun-warmed black grape juice and feel every bit of it trickling inside. I let a ladybird walk over my oiled arm. I can smell the neighbours' long preparations of Sunday lunch. The tension of the argument builds up. By the time they sit down to eat they are threatening, 'Eat it or else.' They shout at May. The husband walks into the garden in anger, sees me, walks back.

My food cravings are bearable now. Food has become something positive for the first time. I can choose to eat what is good for me instead of feeling a slave to what I don't want.

I stop writing to Grey and write for myself. With crayons I do a pale green tree rising from grassy earth with red flowers around it. This is me now. The sun is kissing its boughs. Once I did a tree in black charcoal. The roots had nothing to grow from. It had many branches but no leaves, looked dead and was surrounded by a barbed-wire fence. Somewhere above it was a star. Now the star has come down and become a sun. I oil myself and do self-hypnosis in the sun. In the mist and cold of before, roles didn't touch me. I didn't believe I was a 'mother' and no one else did. Because I didn't 'look like' one? So I escaped that.

I have a dream in which Grey says quite simply and clearly, 'I want you for sex and peppermint tea.' The dream stays in limbo for a while.

'Ah, virgin hair,' says Allsop, the hairdresser. He's about to colour my long, brown hair.

'What's that mean?'

'Never been dyed or treated.'

We drink herb tea. He says, 'I've started giving massage to guys.'

He answers the phone sounding like a girl. We giggle. This time he tells me of his ex-boyfriend and he's more relaxed.

I remember a dream about being black and bleaching my hair and being just about to put a pink tint on it and seeing my head in my dream like a strawberry-coloured cauliflower. This is the next best thing to being black, I think. Anyway, now I like being white I'm starting to look at white people more.

In Blodminster, Gillian tells me about her one and a half tits and the history of what doctors have done to her. When she's gone Amanda says, 'Describe some of your men, go on.'

'There's only one guy.'

'But all the ones that come round. There must be some dishy ones.'

'Pardon?' What is she talking about? I've forgotten about work. I try to remember a client to describe but I can't, so I improvise someone muscular and blond, which seems to please her.

Home at last and the evening sun shines on me. I lie and talk to May in the garden, and oil myself. I test my newly coloured hair against my newly coloured body. The papers say Big Ben has stopped. My eating is just about controlled. I suppose I should enter the world but I don't want to live with Grey or Henrietta.

On the phone, Grey says, 'You turn me on just talking to me.'

That sounds too much like work. He talks about how his wife used to like being tied up. It sounds just like work. He's never really got beyond what I do as everyday work.

Next time he comes round, again he says, 'Let's live together,' and I catch myself 'feeling like a prostitute' when he leaves.

A client leaves and I smile and feel purified as usual.

It's hot and beautiful everywhere. Samantha and I walk barelegged down Foursome Road. I get groceries for Henrietta. In the shop Henrietta is shouting at a customer, 'If you don't like my prices then get out of my shop!' But then she stands looking empty of something, watching the people go by and hoping for a customer. I wouldn't like to have to solicit like that. She pops little gifts into a lady's basket to seduce her further. Her emotions get tangled with the customers' money. They make her bitter. 'They give me bellyache and make my back hurt,' she says to me.

In the hotel in Frillingford I said to Grey, 'Here out of the room it's like the first time I've had sex for two years.' He put a doctorlike expression on his face and said, 'Will you perform a small service for me? It's so nice.' He lost the moment and I see now that sex for him is no more than everyday working life. He can't go beyond that.

'I think what you need is a prostitute, so why pretend this is anything else? If you tell me that's what you want, that's fine if that's the truth,' I tell Grey.

He looks hurt and protests.

'Hmm. But that's what I feel like with you and I've never felt like that before with anyone.'

Phone call from Grey. He sounds nervous, hysterical. 'My kids are the most precious things to me, the most precious things I have, the most precious things I have.'

Release, relief. I've been saved, and he's broken out of it. I'm free, free to get on with my retreat and complete it.

I say to Henrietta, 'If I go to court about my kids, can I say I work for you in case it's necessary? I don't want to say I'm a secretary, as Grey suggested. I'd feel degraded even pretending I had a job like that.'

'Yes, maybe, but I think you should invest some money in the shop and perhaps do some selling for me. It'll do you good.'

'But I'm already being done good.'

'Well, perhaps just some money. Let's go back and discuss it.'

At her flat the phone rings.

'Oh yes,' she says, 'do come round.'

'I'll go,' I say.

'Stay, stay, you must meet Donnie Dalmatian.'

Donnie wears old denim and has a rattling knapsack on his back. His angular face is grinning. 'We might be bugged, you know.' He hacks rye bread with a beautiful knife and proffers peanuts.

'No thanks, really.'

'Oh, little Miss Pure.'

'I do massage, you see, and I'm starting a court case to see my kids more, but it's difficult.'

'You can't do massage, with nails like that.'

'Yeah, I work as a prostitute.'

'Well, my ex-lady has written a book about prostitution. She knows what there is to know about it. She could advise you, maybe.'

'OK.'

He surrounds me with dope smoke while I stroke his beautiful knife and Henrietta talks of her back pains, and soon the top of his head rests against my neck. Henrietta says things about her back she's never said before. I remember a party and the scrunch of crinkling black hair against the side of my neck. This is soft and fair.

'Let's go,' he says, 'to see this friend of mine.'

15

Blunt Finger

'What's your name?'

Well, this is it, I think. I am leaving my retreat to be with him.

'Melissa.' The intimate vibrations as I let him call me by my new name. We go through the first thunderstorm. The sunshine has ended.

In his nicely ramshackle car Donnie talks about his feelings for me, and I look at the hair formation around his mouth and watch the body language of our limbs and the wafting dope smoke.

'It's not the dope. This is for real. I live in Hampstead. It's magic. You can make eye contact with people there. Where do you want to go? I'm not really one for nightclubs.'

'Just driving about. That's nice.' I enjoy the new experience of being out in the dark with the lights.

'Is that all right? Don't you want to do anything?'

'No.'

'Look.'

He gives me a soft plastic lens and through it the streetlights multiply seven times over, all colours of the rainbow. All the colours of my thoughts, of letters, numbers, are out there.

In a Kentucky Fried Chicken in Westbourne Grove, Donnie gets chicken and kisses me with a wide grin, and I eat coleslaw. As we leave, three black guys with brown wide-brimmed hats come in.

'Did you hear what they said?'

'No.'

'Could cause a race riot. Maybe you should be veiled or something.'

In his ex-lady's flat in Hampstead, I look at her grubby, voluminous, ethnic dress and feel the discomfort of her legs enclosed in too tight boots. Her nose is sweet. I imagine Donnie kissing her soft nose. As I sit on the floor, I see the body language Donnie and I are making. Donnie is putting me on display to her. She sits there in trendy untidiness, talking of her cats peeing, her book on prostitutes. She writes on mental health. She is younger than me but has become a grown-up. She is corrupted by qualifications and the job, for which she has been bloated by a large unhealthy banquet. At twelve I vowed to be a virgin of qualifications, exams and machines, to be pure. Donnie shows me her book. At the front is a photo of her when the rest of her was nearly as nice as her nose. I flick through the book.

'What do you think of it?' says Donnie.

'Well, it's just about it being a job,' I say.

'And?' says Donnie.

'Well, there's not much else to say.'

'How's that guy in Broadmoor you have to write to?' Donnie asks her. 'I think he's infatuated with you.'

It hits me in the heart. Both of them secure in their tatty trendiness making the poor bugger into an object. There are books on love and philosophy around the walls. They see through only one face of the mirror, know nothing about how to create love from fucking on dirty linen in the gents' loo at a state mental hospital.

Each cigarette that Jed gave me was an act of love, each cup of tea a dedication. At the hospital, living with the fear of being confined for ever and turned into zombies, we created security.

Two days later. 'Hi, it's Donnie. I've been ringing and ringing you. I thought I'd got the wrong number. I kept checking with Henrietta. Wow, your voice, it sounds as if you're coming from every orifice. When can you come round? Come now, as soon as possible.'

A minicab to a dark flat in a corner of Hampstead Heath. With a wide conscientious grin, he bolts all three bolts on the door of his room. The windows are barred. And now I'm in someone else's domain. The room is full of incomprehensible, complicated shelves and cupboards which hold too many books on the walls. He puts on music. I look at his denim-covered, crisscrossed legs. Through the bars, the sky is dark. He pulls off my jeans. Sex at night under his domestic duvet with a pattern on it. Rough sheets and the rough voice of a country singer. His eyes penetrate mine. His grin is wider and wider. I feel my face go sad. I wonder why. I do self-hypnosis in his blue eyes.

'I vowed I'd never say it again, but I love you.'

'Love you' comes out of my mouth. And we envelop each other in every conceivable kind of cuddle. Nothing of me is outside this. He enters my new body African style. He's naked inside me, naked skin inside mine. I focus completely on a single individual and I let my head rest in dreamed-of places. There are bars across the sky. And I feel myself letting myself get closer to someone else than before.

I go to the loo in his tatty dressing gown. My face looks different from in the mirror at Peachy Rise. On the way back I say Hello to his flatmate. As he is looking at me, Donnie comes and grasps my newly coloured hair.

'I wish I had a pleasing body image,' he says. He won't let me touch his hair. He takes off my bangle and ring. 'I don't like these on in bed.' He looks at my toenails. 'I don't like nail polish either. It's bizarre.'

'I do.'

'I've never experienced it before,' he says, 'but I read about it in a book called something *Marriage* by Dr So-and-So. A sort of sexual electricity that occasionally occurs between two people. Wow, it's amazing!'

'Oh.' His books crowd in on me from their shelves.

'What sign are you?'

'Scorpio. With Grey Flannel it was the other way around,' I say. 'He asked me first how much money I made, then my sign.'

I ask Donnie what he does.

'I'm a telephone operator with the GPO.'

'You don't look like one.'

'I work nights, sleep days. Well, it's just a wank really, just like your job. Not much bread but the hours are good.'

In the mirror I look at us and him looking at us. Never been with anyone who looks anything like me before. I eat more of his peanuts and drink more coffee, get a craving for more food and want to be by myself.

'Won't you stay? Will you stay the night?'

'Yes, some time.'

I regain the room. It looks cold and neglected. I turn the heat on, get into my sleeping bag till the next morning. I am myself again.

Next day I look in my mirror and merge with the room. It's warm again and I'm at peace. And work is a vast expanse of purity, the vast collective prick in the lamp glow.

The ceiling is high and I'm free. Kisses, cuddles, and my mind roams the ceiling. A client's shoulder in double vision making the lamp's shade soft and liquid. Dark winter has started. Sometimes they think it's personal, sometimes for them it is. I avoid touching hand to hand, eye to eye, so that it is pure and uncluttered, skin, bones, hair, muscles, breath of a group. I sigh with peace.

'You look different,' says a client who's been many times before. He looks inquisitively at me and I put my arm round me so he can't see into my private life. Enclose him in a rubber. I notice that I wait until a client has gone before I adjust my bra strap. It's too intimate a gesture for clients to see.

'Do you have a baby?'

'No.' To protect my privacy.

'Well, I can understand someone doing it if she's got to support a kid.'

'Oh.'

'I expect you just do it for the money.'

Think. I just did it because I wanted to. I keep my luck to myself. I feel guilty that I'm so lucky compared to the doctor, the lacemaker and the telephone operator.

After each appointment, 'Why are you giggling?'

'I'm just smiling.'

My wholesale supplies of Durex don't arrive. A form says I have to ring a Neasden sorting office.

'Umm. I was expecting a parcel,' I tell the guy at the other end.

'Oh, expecting, were you, love, huh, huh.' They all sound pissed. I decide to leave it.

The phone rings. It's Donnie.

'I need you. I need you. I need you.' He distorts my time. I want to rest. I shower, put on clean outside clothes, take time to drop my habits from work. I get a minicab to Donnie.

I let all his smells enter me. I reach out to touch him completely. He won't let me touch his hair or face. He squeezes my face with his hand. I wince.

'Ah ha, you're hand-shy.' The blunt finger points. Maybe it's blunt from too much pointing. 'Look, look, I've papered some drawers for you to move in.'

I look at them. I can see my things getting lost in the complication of his room. But it's my duty to be with people. He takes my left leg and pulls it.

'Ha, you've got a problem there.'

'What?'

'You've got a problem there. I started to train as an osteopath. Oh, I didn't finish the course. I couldn't afford it, but I gave a talk on joints and mental health, and they told me it was the best ever. I see myself as a healer.'

For the first time I feel like an object.

'That feels like being an object,' I say.

'I don't put you in any role.'

He tickles me. I giggle and shriek.

'I don't like screamers.' The blunt finger points. 'What you need is body contact.'

'Well, I get a lot of that, you know.'

'Ah, but is it the right kind? We in the West don't get enough body contact.'

He reaches above his mattress and I admire his arm, which is curvaceous compared to his functional legs. He grasps a highly decorated book from the uneven shelf and points his finger at me.

'One must first achieve power before one can achieve

love. Power first, then knowledge and after that comes love. Have you heard of Sufism?'

'Who's Urbidou Beg?' I ask. He's very prominent in the books around his walls.

'Urbidou Beg is the great Sufi leader. I heard of him when I was living in California. I'd read about him since I was eighteen and then one day I knew I had to join him. I sold my house and came over to England because I heard he was here. I joined his commune in Surrey. After two years he threw me out. I write to him but he never replies. I know he threw me out because there was work for me to do out here. This is why I stay in this country, because he is here and I must find that purpose. Look.' He shows me a photo of him in the flyleaf of a book. 'I know he looks like a typical guru but he's not. He's not like anyone.

'If you love me you must love my dog, that's Sufism. But when we talk on the phone, never mention them by name. You have to be careful on the phone. As James Cameron said, "Never talk specifically unless you are in the middle of a field."'

At work a client analyses why he finds it exciting to see a woman belching. 'It's the release, like orgasm, I suppose. I've seen *Soldier Blue* six times. That scene where Candice Bergen belches. Incredible.'

Next time he comes along he has a hard object in his pocket. He strokes it with anticipation.

'Er . . . would you like some, er, Coke first?' he says shyly. 'It'll help you belch.' I smile at Coca-Cola, the fetish object.

Who are the Sufis? What are they doing?

'Ah, they're all about, in a subtle way. They are getting stronger for what is about to happen. I can sense the feeling on the streets. You should move from where you are. There are terrible vibes in Peachy village.'

'How do you mean?'

'There are terrible vibes. Things will happen there first when the bad things happen. Hampstead is the place to be. I want to be prepared. When the time comes you should be here with me and join me in my work.'

We walk through Hampstead. I get cravings for food, but not as badly as before. 'It's like a village,' he says, grabbing eye and body contact desperately. He starts talking to people whenever he can. He takes my hand to get a good dose of what he needs. He says Hello to a woman with a big newly washed dog and a little girl. He looks self-consciously into the dog's eyes as if he's sending it vibrations. The dog turns away. He grasps the little girl, lifting her high in the air, as if spontaneously. She screams.

'I don't like screamers.'

We visit people he says are 'marvellous' and 'wonderful'. They don't have lace curtains over their windows. They sit in rooms naked to the public gaze and on their bookshelves are books on Urbidou Beg. Karen, his ex-lady, had Urbidou Beg on her shelf too. The winter is darker. Who are Sufis and who are not? They all look the same. One guy could have been a client of mine. Would I know? Would he know?

I get exhausted, the way I used to before. 'What do you think of self-hypnosis?' I ask Donnie.

'It's just a technique,' he says. 'Sufism is not a technique.'

Something is taken away. I get weaker. I can't do self-hypnosis any more. I don't do my yoga exercises. When I'm with Donnie I feel myself disappear. Hampstead, London and people become sinister. By myself I smile,

live again and can talk to people. Peachy village, my
part of London, is OK but he won't let me stay there.

'I'm just not one for nightclubs or anything. I like to
see my friends in their homes. Many things are happening now. I expect you go to nightclubs, you look as if
you do. I suppose you always go out with well-off
blokes. What do you see in me?'

This strange image hits me.

'No, apart from Grey, I've never known people with
money. But he was a client. You see, I've been in retreat
for two years. I haven't had a social life. Before my
retreat was another world.'

'Retreat? A Catholic retreat?'

'No, it's just something I did, something for my
good.'

'So what sort of blokes do you go out with?'

'No sort. No one during the retreat, and Grey was
really a client.'

'So I'm the first?'

'Yes, obviously. In my life before, I had an agonizing
craving for food, just like an alcoholic for drink. Once I
started eating I couldn't stop.'

He grins avidly. 'But you're beautiful, slim.'

'What I am has never been what I look like. It put a
cloud, a blot on my life. Being by myself and secure for
two years, I got the eating under control for the first
time and my body felt comfortable. But since I've been
with you it's started again.' As soon as the words are
out I regret them. 'Let me finish the retreat, just let me
have a few days by myself, then it should be all right.'

A reprieve. I smile inside.

'Just before I let you go I'll give you something. Relax
on the bed.'

He takes my head, moves it round to the left. I hear
cracks like shooting stars.

'Will you do it the other way?'

'No.'

Lover turning into an osteopath.

Back in the room the peace is disturbed. I don't feel alone. Donnie's needs are pressing in on me. A Post Office card is pushed through my letter box. On it is written 'I . . . you', signed 'the stitched one'. He phones later and explains. He's crashed his car, and had to have stitches.

The next evening I walk back up the hill with potato patties from the Kentucky Fried Chicken. Donnie is waiting outside on a motorbike.

'I thought you weren't supposed to be eating that stuff? Please let me come inside. Only I can help you. Please let me help you, otherwise I feel impotent.'

In the room. 'It's weird. It's bizarre. It's like a 1930s underwater lagoon.' He adds a chill to my room and distorts it. 'How much do you earn?' I give him a random figure.

'I wish I could buy things for you.'

He grasps my hand and holds a second crash helmet in the other. I see him buying me rings and bangles which become manacles. But I go with him.

'Have you locked your door behind you?'

He revs up his bike and I recognize its sound. I can tell it from a car or a bus now. All traffic sounded the same before, and I used to see other people turning their heads because they knew which direction a bus was coming from. I used to get it wrong. As I sit on the back of his bike I feel its sound. Donnie tells me, 'Don't move with me. Just let me move.'

When he has tied up his bike, locked it, bolted the front door, bolted and barred his room, he puts on the stereo behind his bed. 'It's Led Zeppelin, amazing, marvellous, wow! "Stairway To Heaven". Excuse me, my flatmate's just come back. I must go and flash my bandaged prick.' He goes out and comes back. 'The stitches will have to stay in for another week. Perhaps we could make it with a Durex.'

But I know I can't. Rubbers are part of work. To use one with him wouldn't be honest to him.

I tell him I feel weaker. I've had colds. I'm tired, exhausted, and the overeating has started again.

'Why are you eating? Why are you eating? Ah ha. I know what's wrong with you. I can tell you what's wrong.'

'What? Tell me.'

The blunt finger points. 'Stairway To Heaven' gives me stomach pains. I start to cry.

'Ah ha.'

'When I was twelve I fell off a horse and hit my head on a tree. I got concussion. I was very weak after that. My voice was weak, everything was weak. I wasn't even strong enough to serve with a tennis racket. I started having food cravings then.'

'You think it's that simple? You want the easy way out. Ah ha. You should be eating meat. If a vegetarian mixes with a meat eater, they become drained.'

'When I stopped eating meat I became stronger. That doesn't follow.'

'Ah, you think you did.' The blunt finger again.

The bars, the locks, the pointing finger. I get lost in crying. There's a little peach-coloured velvet pillow on his bed. I stroke it. 'This is beautiful.' The pillow gives me comfort.

'Ah, you can't really be sad, then. You're devious. I must break you of your lifetime deviousness.'

He stops his bike at McDonald's whenever possible and tries to force burgers on me.

'I'd be lost without them,' clients say as they anxiously reattach themselves to their car keys after sex. Through the curtain, I see a formerly carless client climb into his small grey object. It lessens him for me.

On Donnie's bike we pass a church whose notice says, 'Come once, come again.' I must remember to tell that to clients!

'Don't direct the bike,' snarls Donnie. 'Just let me do it.'

He stops at a newsagent's to buy tobacco. It's one I advertise in. This act changes the place for me.

He talks of planning our future. 'You could be a sexual healer. Wow! You could get a decent place in Hampstead. You could go upmarket, £100 a night. Better class of client.'

'No, that's horrible.' I shudder. For them to sleep with me, spend a whole night, would be too personal. I want to do it my way, connect with clients purely as a group, free from personal favours and feelings either way. My way, I'm not dependent on any particular person or attributes of people. I'm only with the good part of every client. I treat them collectively, equally. The money is always the same. It creates harmony, balance, equality. I'm not going to destroy it.

Donnie plays Urbidou Beg tapes when he gets in from the night shift at 3 A.M. Urbidou is being interviewed by a Radio Three man.

One sentence stands out. 'When people come to me, whatever they say, whatever reasons they give – what they really want and come for is attention.' So do clients.

I can't sleep when I'm with him. His room is full of smoke. Who are the Sufis? The ones with Sufi books on their shelves? And why are they all well off and living in Hampstead? Urbidou Beg is well off too? I look at the bars across the sky.

Donnie is breathing very softly, he talks in his sleep.

To daytime music he says to me, 'I want you to be with me and I want to live in the fast lane of life.' He holds the crash helmet for me and crams an unattractive scarf on me.

He takes me to see an old rock singer who has flu and shuts the door on him.

'Have you ever seen this done before?' Donnie twitches his soft cock.

'I dunno.'

'What do you mean, you don't know?'

'Well, I don't remember everything. Maybe, maybe not.'

'You should clench your cunt and relax it. You should practise that.' He encloses sex in a classroom.

He listens avidly to people's problems on the Anna Raeburn show.

'Ah, listen to this. Only a spade could do something like that. 'Women only bleed.' Wow, oh wow, heavy!' Black is being turned into something other. I start to bleed for half a month at a time. I get weaker and frightened.

'Withdrawn' gets stamped in my building-society book.

In Blodminster, Gillian says, 'You know, the other night, the kids had gone to bed and I was here alone. I turned the telly off and just sat there. It was weird. I don't know what it was but I felt really different. I was doing nothing, just peaceful by myself. It was lovely.'

A client says, 'If we had a relationship I wouldn't hold it against you that you'd been doing this if you got a normal job.'

I rest in the peace of Peachy Rise. But I recognize his motorbike snarling outside.

'Look, I've brought an article from the *Sunday Times*. A lady called Susie Orbach has written a book called *Fat Is a Feminist Issue*, see this article. It's because you don't like your body.'

'But I do.'

'Ah ha, are you happy with this?' He traces my mouth.

'I love my mouth.' I never thought of disliking it. It's happy. He doesn't like his mouth and blames his mother for not breastfeeding him long enough.

'Let's make a trip to California, to my friend who makes the coloured lenses. This guy and his lady, they have a baby. She's breastfeeding him and I asked her if she'd let me suck. Wow.'

'Let me look at the article. I'll try it out. Then, I'll see you.'

'I'll see you on my birthday.' It's November but the leaves are still on trees in this cold weather. So I read the article about eating and decide not to feel guilty about eating, to eat what I want, to find what I need. Then my retreat should end if food becomes OK.

Claude Catsilk. That was when I'd left the world. I promised to see him, now I must. I'm nervous. Should I paint my fingernails? No, there's no time, he wants me to come round now.

'Oh, Clover, you're incredible, beautiful, fantastic.'

'I'm Melissa now. I had a retreat.'

'You took my advice and went ahead and did it? Yes, amazing.'

Eh? I think. What advice? I don't remember advice.

The place is beautiful. He's added red and other colours. It's all done with colour. I admire his flat.

'You've coloured your hair.'

In his bedroom a painting of a coffee-coloured girl and on the wall opposite a naked 1930s lady who looks like Maggie Thatcher as a young girl. On his bright red shag pile I accustom myself to the old movement. I touch him more than before. We see, look at each other in our new colours. I feel I've got beyond him. He comes with a deep sad howl on his new shag pile.

He wants to know how much I make. I show him one of Donnie's coloured lenses.

'I want those lenses. I've contacts. We could set up in business.'

'I work as a prostitute so you can't visit me at my place.'

'Ah.' He adds sophistication to his voice. 'We are all prostitutes.'

I test Susie Orbach's theory as we sit naked in his kitchen and eat tarts with real strawberries and cream.

At Peachy I do self-hypnosis. A week of bell-buzzing and telephone-purring and orgasms all nicely balanced. A sweet guy from the vice squad looks through my porn mags and says they're fine.

Allsop gives me a hug and a kiss as I arrive for my hair appointment. I walk around the flat with pale blue bleach on my hair, watering his plants while he has a bath. A guy whom he's just given a massage to looks worried. I smile. 'I'm just the gardener here.' Allsop's stereo is blaring out. I marvel at being able to live cluttered up with all this equipment. On his shelves little photos of a small whipped bum. We smoke dried tomato leaves.

'No, my knees feel a bit weak, that's all.'

'If you plaited your pubic hair you'd be called a blonde platypus. That was an attempt at a "het" joke,' he says, as we walk hand in hand down King's Road.

He's doing massage full time now except for my hair and his cousin's. He fancies lots of his clients and sex with them is a part of his real life. His personal things and his life are all over the flat for them to see. My personal things are on two shelves in a cupboard preserved from my clients' view.

I tell Donnie that Susie Orbach's theories worked at Claude's. I refuse to move my things to his place. He sits at the foot of my bed.

'I'm not saying this is your last chance. I'll do anything. Come to California for a while.'

His eyes are hypnotizing mine. 'I'll prepare my room any way you want. I'll stop smoking. I won't open any Sufi books. It's an addiction. I think that's why Urbidou Beg sent me away, because I got addicted to his books. But I can direct you, I can guide you. I can help you.'

'With what?'

'Well, I mean, if we were crossing a canyon, I would lead you. You must let me lead you. I can lead you. Either you let me lead you or I must continue my journey.'

'I won't let you lead me.' I wonder where he'll find canyons on Hampstead Heath. I put on my new white sheepskin jacket and lock my door on us. 'Goodbye.'

Donnie rings up. He has been thinking of suicide.

'OK, I'll go to America with you, but I want to be by myself first.'

Christmas Day, but no fast. On the mantelpiece at

Peachy a bottle of advocaat for Allsop's Christmas dinner party. I look at the beautiful yellow. The first time I tasted it, I had come straight out of the bin. New Year's Day. Being driven right through the mist and snow of all London in a warm red car (Jed was the only patient who had a car). Roast dinner in his friends' council flat in Luton and this amazing drink which soothed my cough and flu.

Pinching little sips from a house in Hampstead, making sure there was an hour at least for it to settle again.

A boyfriend bought me a whole bottle when I had a birthday in Clapton. It was the ultimate luxury. But I came down with flu and the rest of them finished it off. I gaze at the beautiful drink and think how my life has changed. Now it's something to buy for someone else – someone I'm not even having sex with. I don't need or want it now. That's freedom. I can just enjoy looking at it.

At Allsop's in Sloane Square are Lady Someone who lived in India at the time of the Raj and Des Dearer, a television designer who's gay. We look at the Christmas tree lights with the plastic lenses. The Queen's speech is on. The lady drinks gin and calls her Liz. Des and I look at her through the lens and give her lots of colours.

At Peachy Donnie rings up. 'I had Christmas dinner with this marvellous neighbour – a stockbroker. He actually invited me to dinner with him. I suppose it's conditioning. But I still have the feeling that this Christmas should be spent with a special person.'

There is a flat I want to buy, but I've already given Donnie money for plane tickets. They're booked, and I've put money in his account for more coloured lenses.

'You think a home will bring you happiness, huh?

I'm not saying things will go wrong for you unless you get into Sufism, but . . .'

On the plane I talk to the guy next to me about *One Flew Over The Cuckoo's Nest*, which he's reading, and show the morning sun through the plastic lens.

'Why don't you sit in my place near the window?' says Donnie. And he starts a conversation with the guy and excludes me. I go to the loo and then to the cockpit and chat with the pilots for a while.

Sitting at a bar in New York, Donnie talking about our relationship being worthwhile because it's difficult and only difficult things have worth. A guy drops a packet of cigarettes as he leaves. I tell him.

'You shouldn't have done that,' says Donnie.

And I realize that I'm in the middle of New York but can't see it because Donnie is in the way.

'Is it warm in LA?'

'Yes, why?'

'I'm getting the next Greyhound there.'

In Columbus, Ohio, the bus explodes in flames while refuelling, and I try not to think Donnie might be wishing it; after that the atmosphere warms up and we start partying on the next bus. Trucks look great at night through Donnie's lenses. In Hollywood, I alight on Jackanory's rooftop and rest a while. He opens his apartment window enormously to the Hollywood sign and sings 'Hurray for Hollywood'. Unsuspectingly, being chatted up over a mango juice on Hollywood Boulevard, I go past the Egyptian Theater to Dalton's bookstore to buy a present for Claude Catsilk. I look at a pile of books in the window, and get kind of hit in the middle with the words 'You've got to write a book' . . . I wasn't prepared for that.

Four weeks later in a plane at Kennedy airport,

Donnie sits in the smoking area and I sit in the non-smoking. When I go to the loo I find a large heavy briefcase there. I inform the steward very quietly. His eyes look nervous and his voice nearly stays calm. In my seat I think of us all being blown up. Well, if we're going to die, there's no point in not being nice to Donnie.

I sit down next to him and he says, 'Well, did you get hustled, hassled, ripped off, lose your luggage? Tell me about it.'

'No, I just left my scissors in El Paso, that's all.'

16
Rape Scene

And the Peachy room surprises me by looking as beautiful and friendly as I'd known it to be.

Donnie's room looks cold. 'You know the end of the world was forecast for yesterday, but it didn't happen,' I tell him.

'I know why you're bleeding so much, I have the answer,' says Donnie. 'It's because subconsciously you don't want to do what you're doing. You want to live with me as man and wife.'

'That doesn't follow.'

I start to buy a flat without telling him – in Hickbrick, far away from Hampstead.

Donnie is involved with his bike. 'I need wheels,' he says. 'It's something I need to achieve to fix myself.'

I take my shoes off and walk on Hampstead Heath and enjoy the feeling of my feet. When I get back he is running along with his bike and jumping on it in the hope that it'll go, but it doesn't.

'Let me show you my favourite tool,' he says, and hands me a heavy object. 'Look.'

It's a silver-coloured spanner with the name Shane on it.

I'll pay someone to wallpaper my new working room at Hickbrick, away from Claude's and Donnie's complicated offers of 'help'. There I can continue my retreat.

'Hello, can you wallpaper a ceiling?' And that's how I meet Shane Screwdriver. He's suffering from a hangover.

'Celebrating, you know.'

He's got strong, wild, anyhow cropped hair and green eyes. I show him the silver wallpaper I've chosen.

'Amazing,' he says. He takes me to a pub which smells dirty.

'I want that room wallpapered and decorated as soon as possible if that's OK. I want to work there as a prostitute.'

'That's amazing, that's fantastic! I'm gay. The first time I had sex was when I was nine,' says Shane. 'When I came, I knew – this is life, this is what life is about. To me it was the meaning of life.' Shane gets another round. I have a fruit juice with lots of sugar in it.

In the flat he says, 'Environment is so important. I want to be creative. Life is being creative. Create a life style.'

He lives in a turning off Foursome Road, a street so different from Foursome Road that it is another world.

The houses are big, tattily old, rented flats and rooms. The place smells of incense and nicotine.

Shane has a crescent-moon-shaped cock. He touches me with a pure impartiality. He talks of 'cocks' and 'men' with lingering sensuousness and excitement and of 'cunts' in a way I've never heard before.

At the family-planning clinic where my coil was fitted they check me in a few seconds and say I'm OK. Heavy bleeding happens, they say.

I go to a nature-cure clinic to see Mr Good. First he studies my posture naked and the way my feet balance me. On the table he asks me to clench and checks the tautness of the muscles. And I notice how much kinder and more personal his request is than when Donnie said I should do it.

'I'm going to examine you internally now.' As never

before. It feels as if he is examining me as I am. In all the others, in pregnancy, after childbirth, in special clinics, I was an extension of textbook diagrams. To cover their fear I was usually enveloped in a white garment. Remember the fear in the doctors' eyes as I walked around half-naked in childbirth.

'Your womb is tipped slightly forward. I'm going to manipulate it. This is what has caused the heavy bleeding.'

'Shall I get up now?' I say.

'No, you can stay there if you're comfortable.' So I do.

It's my last day at Peachy. I've stretched out staying here as long as possible. I put my things together higgledy-piggledy. I don't tidy what is left in the room. It doesn't seem complete.

In Hickbrick I don't get a night to myself. 'Let's do clouds, I'll paint a blue sky and clouds. An incredible environment,' says Shane.

But it feels wrong for me. The first cloud formation is a pair of tits, then lots of little bum clouds. One day I come back and find a strange mysterious dimply arse cunt cloud. And in the streets bums abound for Shane. 'Oh, sweet, sweet. Did you see that? Did you see that?'

'What?'

'They're lusting after you. They want to make up to you. I love young straight guys, guys who think they're straight. I want to turn them on . . . to everything.'

Outside Granny's Ice-Cream Parlour in Notting Hill I nudge him and point at the brightly coloured giant ice-cream cone. We giggle. I've started to notice neighbourhoods being different, the décor inside, the difference between ancient and modern, shapes of roofs, stained-glass windows.

At the nature-cure clinic, Wane Waters works on my left hip.

'I used to put my weight on that leg, when I didn't like myself much.'

On the table, I – the object – observe the subject. The osteopath is not so happy working as I am.

'It's amazing how people can grow and change,' he says.

'This guy – he was into Sufism. It was very frightening. When I was staying with him I couldn't sleep. I felt drained. What is Sufism?'

'A weak man can sometimes weaken a strong woman.'

'What is Sufism?'

'It's nothing to be frightened of. It's about love, really.'

'Oh. It didn't seem to be like that.'

Shane says, 'I'd like to have an ongoing relationship with you.'

'Yes.'

'That makes me so happy.'

Henrietta says, 'What does it feel like to own your own place? Your own home, your own property?'

'It doesn't feel like anything.' Peachy was my own place.

Donnie arrives.

'Anything special happened to you?' he asks.

'No, not really.'

'I won't be able to do any work here for a while for you. I have a very heavy commitment to a lady. She's forty-three and she has a big house and a Bentley. But it's not because of the house and the Bentley. What is happening in your life?'

'Well, I'm having an affair with a gypsy. He's gay,
too.'

'Ah, well, you're probably latently gay. You don't
regret it? That we split up?'

'Oh no.'

'What's his name?'

'Shane.'

He looks at me in a certain way, then stops himself,
and I see him wondering at how we can change people
for ourselves. And I know that it will pain him to see
me now that he can't possess me. He gives me lots of
coloured lenses in return for the money I'd lent him.

In the pub with Shane I look at all the faces and the
needs that Shane perceives beneath the faces. All the
faces are hungry.

I mourn the loss of Peachy, I had only what I needed
there. In this pub the grime of the world is getting
closer.

And in bed in the dark with Shane:

'Would you like me if I wasn't a prostitute?'

'Yes.'

'Oh, good.'

'But . . .'

'What?'

'If you see a beautiful man in the street, don't you
fancy him?'

'That's not the point. I was getting right at Peachy,
by myself in a retreat. Even my compulsive eating was
under control. And I know I must get over it, or life's
not worth living.'

The next day I do some appointments. Shane arrives
and has sex with me on my working bed. He's with me
as Melissa in the room where I'm Dawn. He has done
damage but doesn't know what he's done.

The pattern of working is so broken that it hardly exists.

In the morning we walk along Hickbrick Road. There are road drills. Shane ogles the men at work.

I go to see Wane Waters, who lives in a room in a quiet house in Highgate.

'I had a sort of retreat, you know. Life was beautiful in it. It lasted for two years, then I was taken out of it.'

'When I was here at first,' he says, 'no one came to see me for two months. The first time a friend came along it seemed to destroy the place in some way . . . I was working in a fairground. I had to go up to London because of my hair.'

'Your hair? You've got nice hair.'

'No, really, it wasn't. Then I got into diet because of my hair. That led to various forms of health, massage, osteopathy, all sorts of body work.' He unfolds a massage table and I lie on it. He is without his white overall. He puts oil on me. I feel his act becoming more personal, individual.

'At work,' he says, 'some bodies really switch me on. And some switch me off.' I think of Allsop turned on by his clients and letting them merge with and fulfil his sex life. Their work is in the same world as their private life. At work I'm far away from each individual personal thing, in a place they don't know. Wane's massage gets closer and warmer. Who is subject and who is object? My eyes are shut. He is behind my head. His hands are round my breasts. A kiss appears and alights on my mouth. I'm motionless and lying there remembering Donnie D. turning from lover into osteopath.

In his single white bed he says, 'This is the real thing. You see films about sex, but this is the real thing.'

'Oh.'

There is a book beside the bed which I recognize from Donnie D.'s shelf.

'That's a Sufi book, isn't it?'

'Yes, I think so. It's about this guy's spiritual journey.'

'I had a look through. There was only one mention of a woman in it and she had been driven out of her mind. She was in white. That was the only woman in the book.'

'Ah, but Bego the guy is such a good guy. He was looking after her. I've met him. He's really good. She'd been freaked out by a heavy spiritual trip and he was looking after her. She was in a very bad way. Excuse me, you don't mind, do you? I often do this.'

He takes a heavy book wrapped in black silk and sits cross-legged on the floor, unfolds the black silk and flicks the book open at random.

'It's sometimes helpful.'

I read the *Daily Mirror* for safety.

'It's strange. I gave the local bishop a treatment recently. But it was at his place, in his space. It was quite different.'

'Yeah, I know what you mean.'

'He asked me if I was a Christian. I said yes, well, I am, I suppose. Among other things. He didn't pay me, and at his place, I couldn't really ask him.'

'Oh, fantasy, fantasy is so real,' says Shane in the night. 'I believe in fantasy. I take fantasy very seriously. Which fantasies do you have?'

'I don't. Things that happen. Having sex outside somewhere I've never been, before dawn. And when the light starts just afterwards. What I want, the only thing I need now is to get over this eating. And only then can I really start my life. I think I'll write something, too.'

'I may be wrong, but I'll guess. It'll be about how men exploited you in the past and now you exploit them?'

'No, they didn't and I don't. Nothing like that.' But I know the story is not finished. I don't know what it's about yet. I'm still in it. Will the ending be what I want?

'Happy birthday.' I give him jubilee pants so the Queen in her coach and horses can ride across his bum.

'She's at the front,' grins Shane. 'She'll have to go across my prick.'

'I've had a letter from Garden Gnome.' Shane smiles. 'He's coming over. An amazing person. We painted clouds together in Sydney. He's a poet and a dwarf and a mime.'

Garden has a strong fairy-tale dwarf body. His face is elegant, Italianate and looks tall. I imagine how different the world must look to him.

'When I was little,' I tell him, 'I made a house for myself by flattening tall grass. What remained became the walls.'

'I remember battles with weeds.' He grins. They smoke dope and look at his poems, which are full of rich colours.

In bed Shane and I have sex while Garden lies bright-eyed on one side and thunder and lightning play through the window on the other side. Is he gay? Or what? His eyes look brighter. What is he? What's going to happen? He touches me and we fuck higher and higher as the thunder bashes away.

'Everything is too good to be true,' shouts Shane at the thunder.

'It's beautiful, it's amazing,' he says, next day in the

street, as the three of us are discreetly stared at. 'The reality is better than any of their fantasies.'

A client is wearing a green basque and camiknicks which cover his body. I admire the beautiful shade of green and he admires the way I hold my little finger. 'You hold my prick like a teacup.'

We laugh. Then I see how Shane would desire him, need him, and there is no peace. Shane's world is getting too close. I'm squeezed.

Another client says, 'Can you wear some normal clothes, like you'd wear to an office? Pretend you're in an office.' I don't know what I'd do in an office. I look for some brown tights.

A client Shane would give his eyeteeth for, would crave, would desire. I smile when he's gone and start drinking herb tea again.

In the morning I wake thinking of El Paso, and a guy there whose face I described to Shane, to please and entertain him. In the Greyhound bus station I was playing pinball with him. I'd never played before. I beat him twice. I didn't mind if I was winning or losing. Then he said he liked me to lose, so I lost.

And on the Blodminster train I see blond soldier boys through Shane's eyes, not my own. I don't even know if my eyes would see them or not.

At Hickbrick I fold up my silky sheet and put it away. Garden sits on the floor and lights rose incense.

'It gives a good atmosphere. We need something to put the cards on, preferably black or purple.'

I find the black sequined cloak and lay it on the floor.

'Let's do our relationship.'

'From Shane's point of view the first card is the Devil. This is what you want from the relationship.'

'It's beautiful and bisexual. I've always identified with the Devil,' says Shane.

A powerful male figure with breasts and large batlike wings squats on a box. His right hand points strongly down to the earth and to a chain. Two small figures, one male and one female, are lightly chained to it. The rest of his reading I don't take in much. I shuffle the cards for the relationship from my point of view. Garden takes off his cloak.

'The ace of swords. Well, there's no end really. It's a strong card. There is strength there, victory, success.'

Garden opens the window and suddenly appears sitting on the window sill, the sun bright behind him. Distant clouds and painted clouds are all around.

The eight of swords. A woman bound, blindfolded, with a tear on her cheek, eight swords aimed at her but not touching her. I can see it's what the overeating does to me – makes me a slave to it.

The moon card – two dogs are baying and drops of moisture are coming down from the moon. 'Can have a connection with drugs. Sometimes being guided by intuition rather than reason.'

The overeating again. I see myself bound by it.

'And now what you want out of the relationship,' Garden announces.

'Oh, I like that.' It's a card of many mauves and pinks. Someone with a little pack on his back is walking over a bridge towards lovely mauve mountains. There are three stars and a crescent moon in the sky. In the foreground behind him are eight cups.

'Eight of cups. It means changes. The desire for a change. Leaving things behind in order to change for the better. Possibly leaving material things. See, he's turned his back, left his eight cups.'

The last card is the Star. I like the Star. 'The fulfilment of hopes from the gods.' It's a strong beautiful card.

At a male gay disco, guys are embracing bum to prick and Shane wears a bright red silk jumble-sale shirt. We embrace romantically. Garden Gnome is perched on the table. Pete, Shane's only straight friend, is being shown the gay sights of London. 'We're going up to Hampstead Heath later.'

Shane leads through the undergrowth. 'You know the Devil card in the tarot pack? This is the Devil. The Heath is the Devil.' It's so dark, I can't see where I'm putting my feet. I hold Shane's hand in case I get lost. He treads expertly along the well-worn ground. 'I know every inch.' We become separated from the other two. I look up, only the tops of the trees can be seen clearly. Padding feet all around. I touch my handbag. It holds a passport, the few papers I have, and money. I feel the thrill of will-it-get-stolen?

'Through there,' says Shane and I can feel more guys even closer. And they are all round me. They don't seem gay. They are big and pressing close. My jeans are unzipped and I feel a fuck from somewhere. I'm still holding Shane's hand. Not what I expected, it doesn't feel gay but big, butch Irish.

'Why don't you lie down on the grass, love?' That sounds nice. I touch the ground, but there's no grass. It's trampled earth of which Shane has covered every inch in his time. No, I don't think I want to lie down there, my clothes will get dirty. I can't see any of the guys. How do I know if I want to fuck them or not? Hordes of them are pressing harder and harder, closer and closer.

'I thought they were supposed to be gay?' I whisper.

'So did I,' says Shane, below their towering hulks. 'Is it cool?'

'No.'

With an effort we both relax and wind our way out of the hulking tense crowd.

'Wow!' says Shane. 'That could have got heavy!' We walk past them.

'If we hadn't been calm, it could have been really dangerous.'

Near the pond. 'There's a coffee shop down here. It's open late. Everyone goes there afterwards.'

We drink coffee amid lots of smoke. Shane says, 'You don't mind if I go back, do you? I can't wait any longer. Is that OK? I won't be long.'

'Yeah, that's fine.'

I drink more coffee, eat more food I don't want, and think of the scene on Hampstead Heath. In my life before I was a prostitute, I would just have lain down. I wouldn't have known whether I wanted to or not.

Was I ever raped? No, because I was never harmed in any way by sex. From the first time, I knew that it was right.

Sex is Shane's religion but he's chained by it. Though Shane knows his chain better than most people, every sodding bolt of it. I can't take on his chain to please him. I have to break away, break my own chain, which is the craving for food. I can't wait for Shane any longer.

Next day, in the bath, I phone Wane.

'There must be a reason for this food addiction. I must know what it is. I think it's to do with the accident. I was always tired and weak after the accident. Only in my retreat I became strong, started to gain energy.'

'It's the state of the world. People who could help you – the Philadelphia Association is very good.'

'Look, I've had people talking to me. It did no good. It wasted time.'

'Who do you most rely on?'

'Me.'

'Well, then.'

'Bye.'

Shane and I sit on a high wall of a building. Belinda, his little girl, climbs boldly along it. I am motionless with fear of the height and motionless to protect her from fear.

I know what I have to do. I long for Peachy, but I must do it here.

'Look, I'm going to keep to myself, not see anyone till I've got through this eating.'

With no make-up, no jewellery, no watch, clothes I dislike, and my hair muffled in a scarf, I continue my retreat. The phone is on the table but it's still the wrong door for clients to go in and out of because Shane and other friends have been through. And the mirror is the wrong shape.

I start to look at the houses in Hickbrick Road. They are all rectangular. I remember my room in Peachy Rise. The drilling is getting closer, louder.

17
Happy Ending Time

On Capital Radio they talk of spiritual healing at a place called the White Hut. That night I have a dream. Two trendy therapists with Hampstead-American accents are prodding my body. They come to my tits, and the woman says, 'We can do nothing for you.' She points to somewhere far away. 'But go, go to the White Hut.' I go there.

'How did you find us?'

'I had a dream telling me to come here.'

'Sit in front of the healing green light and then someone will come and give you a healing session.' We smile and I go down the steps into the clean and dimly lit sanctuary with white curtains around.

'Take your jewellery off.' But I'm not wearing any now; I've given up jewellery. I sit and absorb the green light, then a middle-aged lady with apricot-coloured hair comes in. I sit upright on a stool with white curtains around and she passes her apricot-freckled hands slowly and peacefully over parts of my forehead, throat, chest, hips and thighs, while I concentrate on letting white light inside me.

The apricot-haired woman talks to me, and invites me to supper at the Starlight Café in Fulham Palace Road. She puts her hands above the food as if blessing or healing it before she starts to eat. I show her one of Donnie's lenses and we look at light bulbs through it.

'It's beautiful. You know, we had a demonstration of Kirlian photography the other evening. It shows the auras that surround every living being and every object. It shows the energy coming from people and things.' She shows me a photo of a leaf – it has colours streaming from it. 'Are you going to come and see us at the Festival of Mind and Body?'

A client is touching me. The drilling sounds louder than ever. I open myself completely to sounds. I can break my own rules. I let the client touch me as never before and let myself enjoy the sounds of the drill. I astrally project myself out of my body further than I have ever done. When I come back to my body I find I'm still sucking his rubbered cock and then I perform a fitting climax for him. Afterwards we shake hands formally and I wonder to myself if he's been before and giggle.

One client accentuates the drama of the situation; another acts as if he believes it's for real. The drills are silent. I let in silence.

At Olympia – the Festival of Mind and Body – I walk around dressed in white past different booths.

And there is Kirlian aura diagnosis. In the darkened tent my hands are placed on the photographic equipment. They lie flat and I feel an oomph under my right little finger. The print is put in developing solution. 'Look at that.'

'There's energy there, but it's not coming out,' says a technician to me. A woman takes my print and I sit beside her. 'There is tremendous creative healing energy here, potential, but you're not really ready to use it. Have you been inside, confined a lot recently?'

I tell her about the eating.

'Why don't you have a physical test?'

At the clinic in Basingstoke they give me water with

glucose in it and take blood samples half-hourly for the rest of the morning. The result will be in ten days' time.

At Hickbrick a massive machine, the worst ever, is coming down the road. Flames come out of the bottom. It belches smoke, filth and noise. It's tearing up the road. It's tearing me up.

What is the opposite of that machine? Classical music?

I take out the little cassette recorder and look at the tapes Shane left. I've never put on music for myself. I find one that says Haydn and put it on. I sit in the lotus position like a triangle. The sounds touch me in my heart, my throat. They are going in my ears as never before. I feel the vibrations through my ears. Then I hear the different instruments. Hear all the different sounds as I did with the drills. It's happened. This is hearing music. Hearing! Now I know anything can happen. All doors are open to me.

Back at the clinic for the result of the test, I lie nearly naked on another table. Mr Georgésa is blond, brown and breezy, back from holiday.

'It's hypoglycaemia, something like diabetes, an imbalance of the pancreas so that eating certain foods, especially ones containing sugar, causes the blood sugar to rise too high and fall too low very quickly. This causes symptoms including insatiable food craving, tiredness and weakness, a feeling of cold. My wife had it for two years. We've only just discovered it. It's a new world for her.'

What to eat and how to eat turned out to be very close to the way I had been eating at Peachy in the retreat. I was told not to take alcohol, nicotine, dope, tea, coffee – the things I didn't really want.

'Was it caused by the accident?'

'Yes, undoubtedly.'

On the bus there are more sounds in voices than I've ever known. I can tell which way voices come from. Someone crackles some paper. It comes from over there. I can hear what all the passengers are saying. It was all blurred before.

Textured sounds make a new world for me, all in stereo. I remember guys talking about their mono and stereo when I didn't know the difference. I only heard mono and saw in stereo.

In Oxford Street I walk into the HMV store. Never dared to go in a place like this before because I was ashamed of my ignorance. Upstairs where the arrow points to 'Classical music'. I buy Deutsche Grammophon cassettes with nice paintings of Haydn and Mozart on the front.

I walk, listening to the sound of it all and lost in happiness.

'Cheer up, love, it may never happen.'

Next day I put Haydn with drills and a pile driver in the background. I write the first page of my story.

Winter gets colder. My body gets warmer, stronger. Every time my blood sugar drops, I notice the symptoms of physical weakness, hunger. I don't blame myself for them and never have them again. I know what they are. I am freed. And I eat as I did at Peachy.

A letter arrives to say that the case of my access has been settled out of court. Bill and Ben can visit me in London.

Next day, after writing, I walk through a park. In a teashop in Hampstead, I meet a woman who starts a discussion about dualism.

'I'm a radical feminist,' she says. 'Bisexual. Though I don't use that word. I prefer pansexual. I mean, I'd fuck a tree if it could be fucked. I wouldn't say all men oppress me, but every man benefits by my oppression.'

'I'm not oppressed.'

'I've nothing against innocence but . . .'

'I had a dream of working as a prostitute and living in seclusion.'

'We all have fantasies,' says the woman.

'I did it.'

Now I have seen the outside, seen their surfaces. If I wanted I could tell what they do for a living, who they 'are', see them through all the many surfaces, and through my surfaces.

They tell us it is the worst winter that ever was since the last time they told us that. I feel very warm. Black refuse bags are piled high against the snow.

In Regent's Park the snow is golden with sunlight. I hear the trees. Can't see the buds but I know they're there. I run through the glowing snow and jump into spring . . .

A selection of sexology books in paperback from Grafton Books

Dr Harold and Ruth Greenwald
The Sex-Life Letters   £2.95 □

Anne Hooper (Editor)
More Sex-Life Letters   £2.95 □

S G Tuffill FRCS
The Sex-Life File   £2.50 □

T H Van de Velde
Ideal Marriage   £2.50 □

Richard Burton
The Kama Sutra   £2.95 □
The Perfumed Garden (translator)   £2.50 □

'Walter'
My Secret life   £3.50 □

'J'
The Sensuous Women   £2.50 □

Edna Salamon
The Kept Woman   £2.95 □

Nickie Roberts
The Front Line   £2.95 □

To order direct from the publisher just tick the titles you want and fill in the order form.

GF3981

All these books are available at your local bookshop or newsagent, or can be ordered direct from the publisher.

To order direct from the publishers just tick the titles you want and fill in the form below.

Name _____

Address _____

_____

Send to:
Grafton Cash Sales
PO Box 11, Falmouth, Cornwall TR10 9EN.

Please enclose remittance to the value of the cover price plus:

UK 60p for the first book, 25p for the second book plus 15p per copy for each additional book ordered to a maximum charge of £1.90.

BFPO 60p for the first book, 25p for the second book plus 15p per copy for the next 7 books, thereafter 9p per book.

Overseas including Eire £1.25 for the first book, 75p for second book and 28p for each additional book.

_____

Grafton Books reserve the right to show new retail prices on covers, which may differ from those previously advertised in the text or elsewhere.